An Outlaw's Reprieve

Quentin Black

ISBN: 978-1-9996006-3-1

Cover design by : Golden Rivet

https://golden-rivet.com/

DEDICATION

Rawthorpe Amateur Boxing Club

AUTHOR'S NOTE

Any specific terms and phrases have
been highlighted in italics and can be
found in the glossary.

RYDER FAMILY TREE

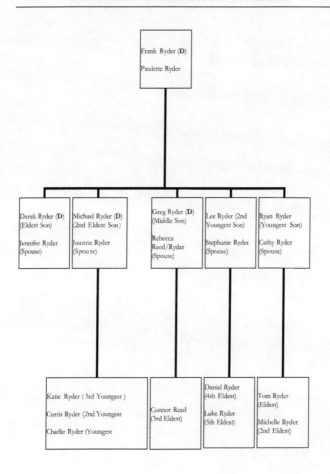

Frank Ryder (**D**)

Paulette Ryder

Derek Ryder (**D**)
(Eldest Son)

Jennifer Ryder
(Spouse)

Michael Ryder (**D**)
(2nd Eldest Son)

Joanne Ryder
(Spouse)

Greg Ryder (**D**)
(Middle Son)

Rebecca
Reed/Ryder
(Spouse)

Lee Ryder (2nd
Youngest Son)

Stephanie Ryder
(Spouse)

Ryan Ryder
(Youngest Son)

Cathy Ryder
(Spouse)

Katie Ryder (3rd Youngest)

Curtis Ryder (2nd Youngest

Charlie Ryder (Youngest

Connor Reed
(3rd Eldest)

Daniel Ryder
(4th Eldest)

Luke Ryder
(5th Eldest)

Tom Ryder
(Eldest)

Michelle Ryder
(2nd Eldest)

ACKNOWLEDGEMENTS

Golden-Rivet for the cover design and promotional video.

The Ings Luxury Cat Hotel for being nice to cats.

Chris Searle for his in-depth and polishing critiques.

And Jake Olafsen and Nathan Hibbert for their always valuable input.

PROLOGUE

'Revenge is an act of passion; vengeance of justice.'

Samuel Johnson

.

1

Paul looked around the half-demolished kitchen, his hands thrust into his hoodie's pockets and his mouth tucked under it.

He stood in the doorway, half in, half out, with the dust from the smashed marble kitchen top mingling with his cigarette smoke.

Brick rubble lay in the corner, together with wood chippings, a pair of styrofoam coffee cups, and cigarette ends decorating the heap.

For nearly a year now, he'd worked for his uncle, ever since being kicked out of senior school.

He'd heard various derivatives of the argument his Uncle Mark was now having with the seventy-year-old widow. Not that she stood a chance—his vastly overweight, but tall uncle was an imposing man against most men, let alone the great-grandma he was now verbally tying in knots.

The scam was to quote an upfront price and get the money in advance for 'expenses'; Mark could have the charm of a car salesman, and old ladies especially seemed to take to him. Upon demolishing their kitchen or bathroom, his uncle would claim unforeseen faults and ask for more money. When they refused, they'd walk off the job keeping the upfront money.

Paul had felt uncomfortable the first few times his uncle had gone through this routine—the angry ones weren't so bad, but those who cried used to make him feel bad. He reckoned Mark would get a fright if any of the biddies agreed to the extra money as he would have to actually do some work.

However, receiving his cut always made him feel better.

Weed made music sound better and Pot Noodles tastier. And having a smoke seemed to be the only thing to stop his girlfriend's piercing screeches and incessant ranting.

Hearing his uncle wrapping up, he flicked the stub into the garden.

"Look, you can either pay me or someone else to do this. I couldn't give a monkey's."

Her timid voice came back with, "But...but...you have my money, so I ca—"

"That money was for tools and materials which I've already bought so I can't give back now, luv. We've spent loadsa fuel money coming over from Hull and turned down loadsa other jobs too."

"But...but—"

"PAUL! WE'RE OFF."

Paul snatched the toolbox and headed through to the hallway, arriving just as his uncle emerged from the living room. He stole a glance in to see the old lady, her face turned white, teetering against one of her pink velvet sofas. Three portraits on the wall looked on—one of her dead husband she'd told them about when they first arrived, another of a beautiful redhead in a black university gown, clutching a rolled-up sheet of paper tied with a red ribbon, and one further into the room of the same woman holding a baby.

He hurried outside and slung the toolbox into the untidy van, closed the sliding door and jumped into the passenger seat as the engine fired up. His feet clanked and rustled against the empty cans of energy drinks and crisp packets.

He saw the curtains twitch as they roared away.

"Fucking hell, how much did we skank her for?"

Mark rubbed his scratchy beard. "Minus expenses. Just over 6K. Not bad, eh?"

"How much am I getting, Uncle Mark?" His curiosity overcame his nervousness towards his uncle, whose body weight was almost twice his own. His uncle's bulging stomach lay wedged between his upper thighs and the steering wheel.

"Ya can have a grand, how's that?"

The knowledge his uncle would pocket the remaining five thousand tainted the thrill of receiving more than he'd ever been given.

Mark slid the van onto the motorway, and soon the blue and white signs indicated they were heading towards their home city of Hull. Paul listened to the forty-year-old fudge the answers to the quiz on the radio, saying them a microsecond after the host and making out he knew them all along.

Paul thought back to when he'd once asked Mark about his conscience when ripping off these oldies. The reply came back laced with derision. *"They've fucking got loadsa money, them. Pensions and families see them right. You saw the pictures in her living room—her family won't be short of a few bob. And those old people are the fucking experts of how to swindle the system."*

Paul glanced across at him. "You ever think that one of these old biddies will know someone—you know, like someone serious?"

His uncle guffawed. "We're the scariest family in Hull—who the fuck is she going to run to? She might have young grandsons or whatever, and all they'll do is talk big words, and after a while they'll swallow it cos they have to."

One of his elbows left the shelf of his belly to root into a bag of Fruit Pastilles nestled in the cup holders between them. He grabbed a fistful and forced them into his mouth.

Paul started tapping his phone to his second cousin, who doubled as his weed dealer. A reply came within a minute. He'd be able to hook Paul up for tonight and Saturday. Paul was happy with that, and would try and pack it in early on the Sunday—maybe about noon—wanting to be fresh for the morning.

There was a big job in Goole on Monday.

Mark's voice interrupted his thoughts as he said to himself out loud, "Who the fuck is that old dear gonna run to? A gaggle from bingo?"

Connor Reed smiled seeing his collar-shirted cousin, Dan, leaning by the Jaguar I-Pace sheltering under the Leeds/Bradford Airport's car park roof.

Connor took off his blue-lensed aviator sunglasses. Though he thought they looked cool, their real benefit was a technology allowing him to see what was behind him with a press of the right temple arm.

As he came close, the narrower-framed investment banker held out his hand formally.

The medium-height Connor, a touch shorter and blonder than the brown-haired Dan, scoffed, "When are you going to stop greeting me like I'm one of your London clients?"

The corners of Dan's mouth raised a little as he fell into the hand-clasp-half-embrace. Connor, more aware of his strength in recent years, did not squeeze too hard.

Though Connor still felt the shrapnel wounds suffered over a month ago when Dan's hand rounded over to his back, it pleased him to note they no longer caused him significant pain. Indeed, they were healing well, requiring just steri-strips as opposed to staples or stitches. The same incident had also dislocated his shoulder, and though its movement remained a little restricted, it had healed remarkably quickly.

"Force of habit."

"Come on, let's get going."

A handful of years ago, Connor had been recruited into the black operations unit named The Chameleon Project led by the shadowy Bruce McQuillan. Since that day, his feet hadn't touched the floor, being on the ground conducting intensive and dangerous operations worldwide. In addition to this, he had become more immersed in the family's criminal empire in recent months.

His surname Reed was his mother's maiden name, not his father's surname, Ryder, which helped keep him under the radar.

The former Royal Marine had arrived back from a whistle-stop tour, checking in with the Ryder family's European partners in various countries, and culminating with a meeting in Craiova, Romania. The consequence of this meeting had been him securing the transportation wing of the family's nefarious operations, opening the opportunity to distribute graphics cards from his contact in Odesa, Ukraine, to the Romanian city.

Before that, he had been away in Italy, conducting a dangerous black flag mission against the

'Ndrangheta and the Mafia Shqiptare, two of the most influential mafias this side of the Atlantic. His roles as both a black operations agent and a fixer abroad for his criminal family could be taxing in the extreme, and he looked forward to some respite.

That said, Dan had just suffered a tragedy, so Connor bolted down rising feelings of self-pity.

Connor's family did not know precisely what he did when he was away. The agreement he had with the men in his family was they were never to ask him—and none did. And he told the women in the family—as he did the taxman—that he managed the European wings of the family haulage firms.

As Dan freed the I-Pace from the slow-moving airport traffic onto the main slip road, Connor remarked, "It's a lot quieter than a petrol or diesel."

"Yep. Still goes though," replied Dan, on entering a roundabout.

He accelerated out just behind a blue BMW Alpina B7 and almost instantly caught it.

"Nice," said Connor. "You staying at Aunt Steph and Uncle Lee's house?"

"For the time being. I haven't lived with my parents for years. I mean, they mean well, but Mum's fussing gets a bit overbearing. It's like she's scared to leave me alone in case I commit suicide."

"That reminds me, did you hear or read about the ice cream man found dead in his van in Harehills?"

"No. What happened?"

"I shouldn't laugh, but he was covered in raspberry sauce, hundreds and thousands, and chocolate sprinkles."

Dan's forehead scrunched. "What…what do you mean? Someone killed him and did that to send a message?"

"Nah, mate," said Connor, looking at him. "He topped himself."

Dan didn't speak for a moment, then threw his head back in laughter and, Connor reckoned, the temporary release it brought him. When he subsided, Connor said, "I'm sorry I missed Angela's funeral."

Dan shook his head. "Don't be. Everyone knows it couldn't be helped. You'd have been there if you could. Besides, the rest of the family were great. Apart from, maybe, Curtis."

Connor felt his stomach tighten. "What was he doing?"

"Not sure. I was preoccupied, but I know Tom had to take him outside to have a word with him. I've heard other things from other people, but you'll have to ask about."

"Snitching tiring you out?"

When Dan simply smiled, Connor continued, "Curtis suffers from Snow White syndrome—he sees himself as a victim and only other people can save him. The irony is Tom has given him ample opportunities to prove himself, and through ill-judgement and a lack of discipline, he's fucked them all up."

"I've not spoken to him much, but he gives off that air of petulance."

Connor checked the following traffic in the wing mirror. "How long you planning to stay up here in Leeds for?"

Dan did not answer for a few moments. "I am thinking of staying."

7

"Why?"

"Several reasons. Mostly, though, there's nothing for me down there now. My family are up here."

"You'll find work without a drama."

"Actually, I am going to set up here myself. The house was paid off, so I'll sell it. Angela also took out life insurance after a particularly bad flare-up with her Crohn's. Put it in my name and—"

Dan paused, and Connor could see it was to get control of his emotions. He reached out and placed a hand on his grieving cousin's wrist, and said with mock-elation, "See, I knew there'd be a silver lining in there."

Dan turned to him with an expression of horror before bursting into laughter again. "How the fuck do you manage to say things like that and still get me laughing?"

"I don't know. It's the intention behind the words, isn't it? Hang on, where you taking me? I'm meant to be dropping my things at Gran's."

"I am under strict instructions to bring you to The Buxton Arms."

"Why? I'll catch up with them tonight?"

"Not allowed to tell you."

2

Paulette Ryder pulled up to her friend's house, relieved to see the silver-streaked, rustic brown hair through the window. This gave way to concern on seeing Rene's slumped posture.

She had not known Rene Lewis long, not even a year, but knew something must be wrong for her friend to have missed a game of bowls.

The recently widowed Rene had come down from Durham over a year ago to be closer to her granddaughter and had joined the newly opened bowls centre shortly afterwards.

It had taken a while for then seventy-five-year-old Paulette—also a widow—to warm to the vivacious Rene, who was five years her junior, but they eventually became close, firstly partnering up and then going on lunch dates.

When Rene failed to answer her calls, Paulette had decided to drive to the house.

After several knocks, Rene's ashen face appeared at the window and then at the door.

As Paulette took in her friend's demeanour, her mind whirred to Rene's granddaughter, fearing the worst.

"What is the matter?" asked Paulette softly. Though she never liked touching, or being touched, by anyone outside of her immediate family, she slid an arm around her defeated friend whom, though only a couple of inches shorter, seemed very small.

"They have destroyed my kitchen, Paulette. I can't even offer you a drink," Rene said, with a shake in her voice matching those through her shoulders.

"Agreed a quote, I did. I paid up front too. After he ruined it all, he told me he was doubling the price— browbeating me with technical words. Thinks I was born yesterday, but he was standing over me and I got so scared."

She choked on a sob, and Paulette's anger rocketed to the top of her head.

"Bastards," she hissed, jolting Rene.

Rene's resignation slumped her next words. "I do have the money, Paulette, but I wanted to save some to pass on to my great-grandson when I *pop my clogs*. I'll have to pay it now—"

Paulette seized her by the upper arms. "No, you fucking well won't."

Rene's mouth fell open. "But, but—"

"And look at me and listen. In a week's time, you're going to have the kitchen you want without paying one penny more," she said, both her cloudy eye and clear eye looking into her friend's hazel pair. "You can't stay here without a kitchen. You're going to stay with me. Go upstairs and pack a bag."

When Rene remained rooted seemingly in a daze, Paulette's finger jabbed to the stairs in time with her words. "Up. The. Stairs. Pack. A. Bag. Now."

This broke Rene out of her trance, and she made for the stairs.

Paulette marched into the kitchen. After staring open-mouthed for a few moments, her jaw set and she tore her mobile phone out of her pocket and began dialling.

Connor's gaze surveyed the empty living room of the new build. After meeting up with his cousins and uncles in The Buxton Arms, Tom had insisted once he'd finished his drink that Connor come with him and Dan for a 'surprise'.

During the meeting at The Buxton Arms, Dan—the only remaining straight-going male member of the family—had declared his wish to be involved in the family business. Connor had managed to convince a reluctant Tom, in the knowledge they indeed needed a talented Investments Manager who they could trust.

Charlie and Luke, two of the younger cousins, had some consignments to oversee and couldn't come for the 'surprise'. Curtis, Charlie's twin brother, had feigned an excuse not to come, but Connor knew it was because he had made him the focus of the party's laughter after catching him out in a lie earlier in the evening.

Tom and Dan took Connor on a tour of the three-bedroom farmhouse out in the affluent area of Alwoodley, six miles from Leeds City Centre.

"All right. What's the surprise?"

His cousins smiled at one another and then at him. Tom answered, "This is. It's your house; at least it will be when you sign these documents."

Dan said, "It's all eco-friendly like you wanted. Solar photovoltaic systems, ground-source heat pumps, underfloor heating and there is a rainwater harvesting system installed."

"How…what?" Connor attempted to collect his thoughts. "Why have you done all this?"

With his work as a Chameleon Project agent taking him all across the UK and Europe, he had not troubled himself to procure a permanent address.

"Because we know you had a lot on your plate, and that you didn't want a mortgage. Dan, here, sorted it out where it's all above board, so it's in your name, bought outright, and the taxman won't be sniffing around, ever."

Dan handed him the documents. "It's true."

Connor speed-read through the papers. If any other men on the planet—with the exception of his black operations boss, Bruce McQuillan—had handed him documents like this to sign, he wouldn't have signed them without a thorough examination.

"I don't know what to say. Thank you."

His cousins exchanged smiles again.

Tom began, "Well, it's the least we could do given—hang on."

He pulled his vibrating phone from his pocket and said, "It's Thatcher," referring to their grandma, Paulette.

"Hello, Gran, guess who I've…all right…right… OK, I'll come down."

As he put the phone away, Connor and Dan looked at their eldest cousin for clarification.

"Some cunt has ripped off Gran's friend for over six thousand. Quoted her for a kitchen refurb. Began the job, demolished the kitchen, then demanded double, citing unexpected costs and labour. That'll rinse the poor mare out—she's putting away for her great-grandson's uni money. Gran is spitting fire over it—I am going to have to shoot over."

Connor called out, "Hey, Tom. Don't be getting yourself, or anyone else tied to us, involved in bashing a set of rogue traders. Given what we're into and how high up we are, the law will piss themselves if they manage to snag you on this."

Tom looked at him with an expression of anger Connor had not seen directed at him for years. "I can't fucking let this go. Some fuckin' heathen is going around our city intimidating and rinsing old ladies of their money and you want me to leave it because we've got too high up? I ain't turning my back on my roots."

"Calm down," said Connor. "I'm not asking you to. Let me deal with it. The coppers' eyes will be on you and Luke and any local enforcers. With me, they don't know when I'm here and when I'm away. It's less likely I'm under any surveillance—believe me."

There were a few moments of silence before Tom said, "I am not being funny, but whereas I would be more inclined to give them a severe beating, you'd probably skin them alive, or take their eyes out and ears off, and that would attract attention."

"Firstly, I am much more imaginative." Connor smiled. "And secondly, I can control my impulses for the greater good."

"All right. You handle them then," said Tom. "Thatcher has taken her friend round to stay at hers until I get her kitchen sorted."

Dan asked, "How's that going to happen?"

Connor and Tom looked at him with frowns, before Tom answered, "We have a construction firm or two on the books. She'll have her kitchen in a week, but it's the principle."

Connor asked, "Where's my bike?"

13

Tom replied, "In the garage, mate."

Dan added, "I heard Gran gave you Grandad's old Speed Triple. You must be honoured, but then she does think you're the Messiah."

Tom sniggered. "Whereas, if she saw either of us walking on water, she'd say it was because we can't swim!"

Dan laughed. "To be fair, I think that bike was to make up for the fact I got given a Spider-Man Web Blaster for my birthday and not Connor."

"That's not that great a present for your twenty-first," said Connor, and they all laughed. He appreciated Tom and Dan not showing any resentment of Paulette's blatant favouritism towards him.

Dan sighed. "Considering the type of things you have both pulled off, these idiots should be a walk in the park."

Fred Troy tapped his gold rings on his desk, listening to his brother's proud tale.

They sat at a right angle to one another on the grey, cushioned sofa. The converted caravan also doubled as one of his offices. It oversaw his favourite business venture—the breeding kennels of pedigree dogs.

Though he kept the dogs out, their barking and the smell of their food filtered in. The small, vintage television, complete with tuning knobs, rested on a shelf above his brother's head. From the screen flickered silent images of a soap opera. On the rickety table between them sat the cups of tea he'd had his brother make.

Fred, the elder by three years at forty-three, was also around three stone lighter than the obese eighteen-stone Mark. Indeed, all the Troy men had excelled in their youth on the local rugby teams around Southcoates East in their native Hull. Apart from, that is, their middle brother, who was a beanpole of a man, despite being the tallest at six-foot-five.

Fred scratched at a gap in his black, thinning, gelled-back hair. He did not feel sorry for the old dear—he could not understand why being old entitled someone to special treatment—but was growing bored of these bragging sessions.

He endured them, with a smile, as he knew Mark looked forward to telling them. And if he rushed over to Fred's dog yard to boast, then it meant Fred got his cut quicker.

"She tried to plead poverty, but I wasn't having any of it." Mark smiled.

"How much you tax her for?"

Mark shifted, and Fred knew he was uncomfortable telling him, but fear would keep him from lying.

"Over six grand. And that old dear doesn't know the police will throw it in the bin, and not even Superman will be getting it back for 'er."

Though Mark could look scary, the truth was that, as a young man, he had been on the receiving end of more than one hammering, which spoke of his lack of ability as a fighter.

Mark had a neck tattoo of two black birds with the words 'The Airlie Birds' between them, denoting

15

the city's Rugby League team. Almost entirely bald on top, with thick hair to the sides, he'd been a decent *prop forward* in his day, but ill-discipline had ended his career before it had even begun.

He had gotten into the 'trades' as a result a long time ago, but Fred would never have had his little brother doing any work in his house. Mark had learned enough to talk like he knew how to do a good job, but if there was a corner to be cut, he'd take it.

Not that he had to ever concern himself too much with reprisals.

"Not bad for three days' work," said Fred, before beckoning with his fingers.

Mark reached into his jacket before sliding a bulging envelope over. Fred did not need to count the money to know the entire nine hundred pounds was there.

Six years ago, Mark had attempted to hold back on him. Fred, and their brother Andrew, beat him up severely in his house before using the tip of an iron to scorch triangles down his spine. Mark never held back or was late with a payment again.

"Young Paul says you've got a few more of these lined up?" Fred watched his brother's face. He would always resent handing over his fifteen per cent, but that gave way to the pride of being an 'earner'.

I can read him like a book.

"Yeh, a few dotted around," said Mark, lifting his chin and wiping the sweat away with his finger. "Fred, what are the dogs you have out there now? I haven't seen them before."

"Those big bastards are Cane Corsos. The Romans had them. They've been used to hunt boar, they are that fucking strong. I've had a few of them trained in Poland, so on my command I can switch them from being docile into ferocious savages whenever I want. The untrained ones are just gentle."

"They fetch a lot of money?"

Fred would usually tell him to mind his own business, but didn't want to deflate him.

"About twenty-five thousand per litter of eight. Three litters a year each. I have a few bitches, too, so it's a tidy sum." Fred watched his brother's thought process on his face. "You working today?"

Mark answered, "It's *mafting* out there, I'm sweating cobs. Meeting the lads for a cool beer."

"Wages come out of your pocket as soon as they go in," said Fred, without disdain.

"It's only a couple of jars."

The older brother knew that meant an all-day session of beer, chasers, cigarettes, lines of coke, a doner kebab, a spliff or two. And once he'd stumbled home, he'd either pass out on the sofa, or force his carcass on his young addict of a girlfriend—probably after smacking her about first.

"I like you're keeping out of Hull. Everywhere else, you go ahead."

"I've got another in Leeds, one in Cas' and another in Donny," crowed Mark, referring to the small cities of Castleford and Doncaster.

"How are you still getting business if you're ripping all the customers off? Don't they check online?"

"Arrrgghhh," said Mark conspiratorially, tapping his temple with his finger, his gold watch constricting his wrist. "Paul knows this brainbox nerd who sorts the website for us. Changes everything over and buys reviews—fuck knows how he does it. Some sort of secret internet. Paul keeps him in weed and that. Phone rings off the hook, summat to do with getting the website to the top of searches, whatever that means. That's the only reason we haven't cuckooed the lad."

Fred knew cuckooing was the one area of crime Mark excelled at, seemingly able to manipulate the weak and vulnerable with uncanny ease. All it took was a little bit of intimidation, and Mark gained access to their homes. And within those four walls, drug dealing and manufacture could begin. His current girlfriend's flat had been just the latest in a long line of drug dens before moving her in with him.

"Best look after this lad, then," said Fred. "Look what happened to our Nat. Coppers are hot on all that internet-based fraud."

In addition to the brothers—Andrew and Mark—they had a younger sister, Natalie. After completing ten of their thirty-month sentence, she and her boyfriend were due out of prison on tag in less than three weeks.

They had conned over three hundred people out of a combined third of a million pounds via their furniture bargain social media page.

The Troy family had managed to warn off most of the witnesses, but enough got through to court. Fred remembered Mark sniggering when one couple told the court they had to sleep on the sofa as their cystic fibrosis-addled son's promised bed had not turned up. It had been stories like this that led to their custodial sentences.

Mark shook his head dismissively. "If he's ever caught he won't have the gonads to grass."

Fred slid a business card over to him. "Right, then. Tomorrow, Andrew is going to pick you up and the pair of ya are going to go to this address."

"How come?"

"Cos I forgot to book the function room at The Tavern for our Nat's coming home party. The gaffer said it's been booked that weekend by this old couple for their granddaughter's graduation."

"Why don't you just tell the gaffer to fuck them off?"

"Because these old folks will raise hell. Their family will go to solicitors and all sorts. Besides, the gaffer pays us protection money—he can't pay us if he's out of business, which he will be if it gets a bad reputation. Andrew will do all the talking. Don't say a fucking thing."

Seeing his last words vex his little brother, he decided to mollify him, and said, "Andrew is going to get a *cob on* with how well you're doing at the moment. Let him be the hero of this."

Andrew was already the hero to everyone in their world's eyes. The second eldest brother not only had a highly profitable loan-sharking business, but had facilitated the entry of firearms and drugs from Holland into Hull to distribute to criminal elements in Liverpool, Manchester, London and Newcastle. They had even made a few runs to Glasgow and Edinburgh. The central Caucasian crime family in Leeds had rebuffed them, as had a couple of the London firms, but business was booming.

However, Mark smiled, visibly mollified, and pranced as he left the office.

Sometimes people are like dogs, Fred thought, *you just need to throw them a bone.*

19

3

Curtis sat in the office, staring straight ahead at the framed Leeds United shirt signed by all the players. The searing feeling he had when Connor embarrassed him for telling a story in The Buxton Arms came back to haunt him when he had time to think like this.

I bet they've all told stories that weren't true in their time. Talk about how family is important, but they gang up on me, laughing.

He listened to the middle-aged Lynn in the other room give her usual spiel. "Incall or outcall? Incall is when you meet the girl at one of our luxury apartments, and an outcall is when she comes to you. Sir? How long? I'll check when she is available. Angel is available from three o'clock this afternoon. It is courteous to have her gift ready in an envelope on arrival. However, you are paying for her time only. Whatever happens within that time is between two consenting adults."

Curtis used to find the last line amusing, as the website's list of services for each girl explicitly stated what the girls were prepared to do: water sports, ATM (ass-to-mouth), anal, oral without (condom), and girlfriend experience being among them.

Imagine if you got there and she insisted on just tea and biscuits.

His thoughts turned back to his situation. He had once been in charge of overseeing the family's domestic trucking operations, and was paid handsomely as a result. After a few disagreements with Tom over his scheduling of the runs and his perceived lack of security measures, he'd been taken off it.

Right enough, Tom had given him this gig looking after the escort agency, but then made him report to Luke. The enforcers who looked after the girls were chosen by Luke as well.

The humiliation had burnt inside and had only got worse.

He knew they'd put him in here to keep him out of the way. He'd made mistakes, but how was he meant to learn? Besides, Tom's paranoia stifled any opportunity to make more profits.

There was no need for them to put him here and take the piss. And he had taken a bullet in the shoulder for them. That he and Charlie were going to inquire about guns behind the family's back was irrelevant—the family did not know to this day that's what they'd been up to.

Curtis knew what he had to do to get respect. And he would have his own thing going on that they couldn't take away.

He would need guys of his own eventually.

Andrew Troy pressed the relevant button on the high-rise tower block's stainless-steel panel. There was no answer, nor did the buzzer signifying the opening of the door sound.

In less than thirty seconds, the face of an olive-skinned youth appeared behind the glass of the door and opened it. He sported a Chelsea football top from a few seasons back, and gestured for Troy to follow. They stopped at a door a little way in on the right, and the Chelsea shirt knocked on the door.

It opened to reveal the sounds of a computer game, smoke and another teen—this one older in a beige shirt, who gave a nod to permit Troy entrance.

The Chelsea top led him down a small corridor to the living room where six men sat on sofas—four watching the big flat screen with one playing a game that seemed to involve driving around streets, then alighting from the car to shoot people.

The scene demonstrated to Andrew just how much the balance of power had shifted. When these Kosovan Serbs first came to him, it had been with hats in their hands for him to lean on certain councillors to secure housing, to provide them with product and to facilitate the illegal arrival into the UK of their kin.

And now he had been summoned to this hovel on Great Thornton Street, to meet 'the boss'.

The man sat directly across from him barked and the game paused, with all other men leaving the room.

The one who had ordered the others out stood. A short but squat man, whose bulk pushed against the grey cotton tracksuit. The large forehead gave the impression his full brown hair was receding. The short, groomed beard underlined a surprisingly cheerful face.

"I Hektor Dekovi. I thank you to help my family and me," said the man, holding out a hand from which a gold watch hung.

"Happy to help," answered Andrew, shaking the hand that did not attempt to exert any pressure.

"Please, to sit," said Dekovi. "Want cup of tea?"

It felt disconcerting to Troy that although Dekovi maintained a cheery expression, his eyes never blinked.

"No, thank you," said Andrew. "What can I do for you, Mister Dekovi?"

"Please, you call me Hektor," said the man, whom Troy knew to be a handful of years younger than his own forty-two.

"OK, Hektor, what can I do for you?"

"We want to now open wings," said the Kosovan, stretching his arms out for emphasis.

Troy felt a worm in his stomach despite anticipating something like this.

He cleared his throat. "Hektor, maybe it is best to wait a while. Maybe it is wise to lay low for a while and get to know the areas a bit more."

Hektor's head nodded mechanically before slowing as if by natural inertia. Then he smiled and said, "Your family have problem with local enemy…rival…yes?"

Troy knew he was referring to the Thompson brothers from Bransholme. Charlie 'Bigga C' Thompson and his brother Nevin had been muscling in, and it had been eating into Troy's revenue.

"Yes. Although it seems to have quietened down in the last week or so. I think the elder brother might have gone on holiday."

Hektor shouted a few phrases in Serbian. Troy's nerves shot into his mouth.

After a few moments, one of the men came in. He held something in his right hand hidden by what looked to be a barber's gown.

Hektor said, "This is present to you," before gesturing to the underling.

The man removed the gown and the shock pressed Troy back into the sofa.

The cut-off face of Charlie 'Bigga C' Thompson stretched over the mannequin head.

"You my friend. I fix problem. I your friend. You fix problem. This is your city. I want another city."

"I understand," said Troy, almost involuntarily. "Maybe I can find you a contact in another city to spread your wings."

Hektor straightened out of the chair with a broad smile. When Troy stood with him, Hektor embraced him before clasping his uppers arms hard despite the height disparity. He looked up at Troy's face.

"We fight any of you…your enemies," he said, beaming, before adding, "Not worry. Dogs will make face disappear."

Connor pulled up in his gran's driveway in the Burmantofts area of Leeds. Despite several offers by the family to move her to a more affluent part of the city, the Ryder family matriarch had always refused. As a compromise, she did allow the complete renovation of her home to the point of being one of the more expensive homes in the area. Due in small part to the security measures, and in large part the Ryder family reputation, it remained free from the threat of burglary, although the area had changed in the decades since she and Connor's deceased grandad had first moved there.

Unlike many of their generation, his grandparents clamped down on any racism, joking or otherwise, in their household. Connor remembered his gran clipping him around the back of his head at seven years old when innocently referring to the corner shop as the 'Paki shop' because that was what he had heard his Uncle Derek call it.

His grandparents' 'Us versus Them' was directed towards the class system; specifically the white and Afro-Caribbean communities of Burmantofts versus the Leeds City Council and national government.

He pressed the iron poppy doorbell.

His gran, straight-backed despite her seventy-six years, appeared. Her light brown hair—grey at the roots—hung shoulder length. Her left eye was ever so slightly clouded and offset.

"Took your time, didn't you?"

"That's what she said."

"Who said?"

"Never mind," said Connor. "Stop blocking the door like some Russian bouncer."

He gave her a peck on the cheek as he stepped in, which he knew she appreciated despite her false scowl.

"Thomas told me he's told you."

"Yeh."

"Now listen 'ere, we in this family won't ever be so high and mighty that we forget to look after our own. I want those basta—"

"Calm down before you give yourself an aneurysm. This is me you're speaking to now. You don't have to fret about what's going happen to whoever is behind this."

Though his tone had a jovial edge, none of the other grandchildren could speak to her in that manner.

"Good," she said, with a grimace of approval. "Back in my day, you could leave your door unlocked."

"Because there wasn't anything worth nicking."

She tutted and ushered him into the living room. "I'll make you a black coffee. Although, I am not sure why you keep having them—it'll stain your teeth in years to come."

He entered the living room. The warm colours of peach and cream made up most of the room, the cupboards and table on the perimeter being made of polished wood.

The lengthy leopard print corner sofa unit drew the eye. A legacy of his deceased nature-loving grandad and, however much his gran claimed to dislike it, Connor knew she would never get rid of it.

On one side of the sofa sat Tom, nursing a white coffee, and on the other sat a smiling lady, who Connor judged to be around her late sixties, grey-flecked rustic brown hair, wearing a white cardigan splashed with colourful embroidery, and a black skirt. She sipped at a cup of tea.

The leather recliner—his grandad's chair—remained empty. His gran would insist Connor sat in it when he visited, but he hadn't sat in it in front of anyone else but her.

The lady looked up at him and called out to Paulette, "Are all your grandsons handsome?"

"And I thought my cataracts were bad," replied Paulette, entering the room. She elbowed his triceps and said, "Sit, you're making the place look untidy."

Connor—not wishing to sit in his grandad's seat in front of Tom—stepped towards the sofa to sit next to him.

"Not there," she crowed, before nodding to his grandad's chair.

Connor descended into it. Though not a superstitious man, the chair did give him a sense of…importance. He gave his cousin a tight smile. He returned it with a wider one. One of the things he loved about his elder cousin was his complete lack of jealousy towards anyone, least of all him. He knew Tom considered him to be the leader of the family, whereas Connor thought the opposite.

"How are you, Mrs Lewis?" Connor asked.

"Now, I'll tell you what I told Thomas: it's Rene, if you don't mind."

"Rene it is," said Connor, before asking Tom, "Where's Dan?"

"He had to be getting back."

Connor knew that meant *'I don't want him involved in anything any more than he has to be.'*

Paulette sat beside Tom, who said, "Rene, after your cup of tea, we are going to go around to your house. We are going to meet a builder—an honest one who knows what he's doing—and you're going to tell him exactly how you want your kitchen doing."

Connor saw her face light up with delight before the expression died as quickly as it came, and he quickly added, "Rene, you won't be paying for this."

"What do you mean?"

"We will be getting your money back. It's a debt recovery," answered Connor. "I need to ask you a few questions."

She looked at him curiously. "OK."

"How did you find out them?"

"I typed in 'kitchen fitters in Leeds', and they came right up."

"What name did they come under?"

"MT Kitchen Fitters."

"Can you give me the telephone number you used to contact them?"

"Oh, it's disconnected now. I've tried it several—"

"I asked for the number, not if it's working or not."

Connor delivered his interruption with smiling eyes, which elicited a smile from Rene. She gave it to him, before asking, "Do you not need to write it down?"

"No," he answered truthfully. Connor, initially through his agent's training and then off his initiative, had developed a sharpened ability to memorise. He had a set of symbols of a similar shape to numbers in his mind. One, two and three were the Eiffel Tower, a swan and a magnet. His brain would zip a story together when told a sequence of numbers, and it allowed him to recall it with ease.

He continued, "And your number?"

"What do you need my number for?"

"To send you nude pics to cheer you up, Rene."

She recovered from the shock quicker than his gran and declared, "I won't say no to that."

"Connor. Really," admonished his gran.

"In all seriousness, it might help me locate them if I have your number."

Rene told him, and he was glad she did not press the issue further. He did not want to explain how his tech geek Cousin Charlie might be able to pull the records with the two numbers.

"Anything else, Mr Detective?" she asked.

"No. That'll be all for now, ma'am."

"Good," said Rene, draining her cup of tea. "Are we off, Thomas?"

"Yep, let's go."

They all stood and Rene extended her hand out to Connor.

As he took it, she asked, "What are you going to do when you find them?"

"I'll give them a stern ticking-off."

She looked at him for a moment before following Tom out.

When the front door clicked shut, his gran said, "They better not ever do this, to anyone, again."

4

Andrew Troy felt an amused disdain watching his brother Mark heaving his overweight carcass out of his van. Not that Andrew had to work or sacrifice to maintain his rake-thin physique. He could go on a week's long eating and drinking binge and not put on a pound.

He watched Mark wipe the crisps' dust from his hand on his trousers, pull his rugby shirt back over his exposed underbelly and shuffle across the pub car park towards him.

Though much heavier, even before piling on the weight, Mark's body language towards him always reminded Andrew of how Fred's dogs would lay and expose their bellies to him.

"Hiya, Andrew," said Mark, squinting up at him against the sun's glare. If Mark stood straight, he wouldn't have to.

His younger brother's hair contrasted with his own; whereas Mark had barely any hair on top of his scalp, Andrew's was a full mop, but—despite being not long past forty—had more silver than its original black. Still, he knew which he preferred.

"Let's go in your van," said Andrew.

The way Mark looked at him indicated to Andrew he wanted to ask why. Instead, he simply nodded under his elder brother's gaze.

When Andrew got in the van, he cleared an area to sit. Empty cans of energy drinks and crisp packets littered the footwells. The car's air freshener, frayed-edged and shaped like a blue tree, hung from the inside mirror and had long since retired.

"Why do you fuckin' live like this? There's shit everywhere," admonished Andrew.

"Time, isn't it. I am here, there and everywhere. Don't get—"

"It's as simple as a carrier bag. Besides, young Paul works for ya. Get him to do it. Smells like a fuckin' heart attack in here."

Mark gave a meek nod. "Where are we going?"

"Head up to Runnymede Way in Kingswood."

When Mark began to reach for the SatNav, Andrew exclaimed, "For fuck's sake, you've lived in Hull for nearly four decades. Don't you ever open your fuckin' eyes?"

"I…I know how to get to Kingswood, just not Runnymede. If you give me the street name and house number it'll take us right there."

"Shut up, you *Twazzock*. If the coppers ever make a link between us and these people, the SatNav history could be used in evidence. Just head up to Kingswood and I'll direct you from there."

Andrew used the time to calm down. Though he knew the quagmire he found himself in with the Serbs had triggered his bad mood, his younger brother's incompetence exacerbated it.

It had been like that since they were kids. As Fred was too old to have been involved with Mark growing up, it had been left to Andrew to bear the brunt of his younger brother's fuck-ups—going into bat for him when he'd *gobbed off* at people he shouldn't have.

Like a stupid Jack Russel yapping due to the protection of a Pitbull.

Andrew had asked Fred why they kept Mark involved in the family businesses with him being such a liability. Although Fred had made the valid point they should keep him close to limit the damage he could do, Andrew suspected his older brother had a soft spot for Mark.

And he also reckoned Fred secretly enjoyed pairing them up together on occasion, knowing how riled Andrew got.

He observed Mark's body language out of the corner of his eye and decided to lighten the atmosphere.

"Fred said you have a tidy set-up going at the moment?"

His younger brother's face began to brighten cautiously. "Yeh, it's going well. Got all my ducks in a row like you taught me."

"Well, don't go getting lax."

"Nah, I won't. I am on top of it," Mark stated proudly.

Andrew began directing him towards their destination before stopping them on a classy suburban residential street.

"Now then," Andrew began, "go down this snicket. It's that end house. Reach over the top, catch the bolt and let ya'sen in. Give them both a scare but don't go too far. And, they have two Yorkies, so use your imagination. And for fuck's sake, tell them why you're there—that they are going to pull their shindig at the club."

"Fred said you were coming to speak to 'em?"

Andrew smirked. "I did. Last night. Got all togged-up to look respectable and they fucked me off. So, now you're here. So, tell me exactly what you're going to do."

Andrew held his temper as Mark initially stuttered through the plan. On his third reciting, he got it correct, and Andrew made him repeat it twice more.

"Go on, leave the keys. I'll drive."

Mark nodded and got out of the van. Andrew envied his younger brother's skip as he got out.

He'll never have to worry about anyone truly dangerous like I do.

Connor stood on his outside decking while sipping a coffee. Not long after five o'clock in the morning, he could only hear the birds of the meadow before him.

In the distance, the sun had begun its slow climb over the far treeline, scattering sparkles across Eccup Reservoir. He had researched that 'sky-watching' helped stimulate ideas and creativity.

He felt a weird revolving interplay of contentment and anxiety. Contentment, as even though he had enjoyed the quasi-nomadic lifestyle of hotels and safe houses, he finally had some roots for the first time in many years.

Anxiety, as having a fixed abode now made him vulnerable to enemies. Paper trails—digital though most would be—would lead back to this place. He had already asked Jaime—the logistics and intelligence backbone of the black operations unit he worked for—about fitting his house with the relevant security measures a man like him might need.

And though he felt grateful in the extreme Tom and Dan had done this for him, he also felt a pinch of emasculation—*Other men bought your first house for you.*

He quickly admonished himself—*Only you could have a beautiful house bought for you and still find something to complain about.*

He fleetingly thought this might have been a home he could have shared with Grace. The house and area would have been worthy of the wage she commanded at the hospital as a surgeon.

The last time he had seen her was when he had rescued her from the twisted megalomaniac child-murdering psychopath who had kidnapped and held her in Ukraine over a year ago. It had been then when she had seen the side of him only a few people had—his love of torturing evil people. And it had been then she had issued him the ultimatum to give it up—one he refused.

Whenever feelings of regret began to ice his heart, his brain would thaw them out. He remembered his dad's advice on women he had given him when Connor was around fourteen. He remembered it because it had been on a drive back from Birmingham after Connor had won a match against a former ABA national champion, and his dad's pride had made him more verbose with Connor than usual:

"Young love is the first time you get a rush of chemicals anywhere between the age you are now to your early twenties. Just be careful of getting yourself tied into anything like a marriage, mortgage or kid when hit by it."

"How will I know I have been hit?"

"Because you'll enjoy having deep and meaningful conversations between having roll abouts. You might even find

*her funny. It'll last around two years and that's when you have
to have a serious assessment. Despite what your grandad tells
you about just finding a sweet girl who will do the chores and
not fuck about, it isn't the fifties any more. The question you
have to ask yourself is not 'Do I love this woman?', it's 'Am I
going to be satisfied with the life I am likely to live with this
woman?'"*

"If you love someone, shouldn't you stick with them?"

*"No! You can love someone but hate your life with them.
If you're the sort who craves different experiences—travelling,
danger, kinky sex, drugs or whatever—and she's the quiet life
type, it's going to be a problem. One will resent the other, and
the other will resent being resented. A big one is kids—one
doesn't want kids but the other does. It's more if the woman
doesn't want any and he does that breaks them up, because if
the woman really wants them there is always the option of
'forgetting' to take their contraception."*

"What if you have weird things that make you happy?"

*"There're well over six billion people in this world and
there's the internet, something that Ian Brady did not have but
still managed to meet Myra."*

Connor drained his coffee and snapped back
into the present—*Even if Grace accepted me for who I am,
her being with me would just be putting her in danger, and any
kids if we'd have had them.*

He turned back and washed out his empty cup.
He had his morning routine of exercising, mobility
work, a cold shower and studying to complete before
his younger cousins Luke and Charlie arrived.

In the living room she'd shared with her husband, Jeremy, for twenty-two peaceful years, the sixty-six-year-old Emily would have resembled a kneeling gargoyle had it not been for the shock and empathic pain choking her and the way her fingers shook.

Her Yorkshire terriers, Benson and Hedges, were frantically licking her sixty-eight-year-old unconscious husband's face, as *The Chase* played in the background. Hedges did so despite his broken hind legs by the monster who had punched sixty-eight-year-old Jeremy to the ground after her husband's futile effort to protect them all.

Before the animal had left, he had seized her by the throat to hiss, *"If your granddaughter's party isn't cancelled, I'll be back to break both of youse two legs and skin those fucking dogs alive. Don't think you can run to the police, they can't protect you from my family."*

With that he had dropped her to her knees, from where she now knelt, paralysed.

Jeremy groaned, which thawed her catatonia, and she scrambled towards him. Clasping his face, she saw his eyes open with pain and confusion.

5

Connor opened his door to reveal two of his younger cousins. Luke stood as a little taller and a slightly better-looking version of himself. 'Cool Hand Luke' had been their grandfather's sobriquet for him, whereas their Uncle Michael's nickname for him had been 'The Aryan' on account of his bright blond hair and blue eyes.

Behind him stood Charlie; about Connor's height, with brown hair, as opposed to his own sandy-blond. Charlie had a slighter build to the lithe and athletic Luke.

"Finally got your own gaff, eh." Luke smiled.

"I have, so remember to take your shoes off."

He gave them both the hand-clasp-hug as they entered.

Luke turned right into the living area and exclaimed, "Fuck me, it's massive. It's begging for a pool table in here."

A dark green leather settee patrolled the room's perimeter; he would've preferred a velvet one, but in the end opted for the easier-to-clean leather. A coffee table with an underslung drawer unit stood close to the edge of the far right end of the sofa.

"Not got a telly yet?" asked Charlie. "Unless it's upstairs?"

"No, and I am not getting one," said Connor. "The only sources of entertainment I have are some fiction books, a chess set and a pack of naked playing cards—naked girls before you get too excited."

He led them into the kitchen, took their coffee orders and within a few minutes they were sitting around the light grey marble top with blue swirls in it. Cream, black, wood and earl grey made up the rest of the room.

Connor asked, "Did you find anything out, Charlie?"

Charlie had developed an interest in computers just before he had hit his teenage years. Now in his early twenties, he was perhaps the most crucial cog in the family business, behind Connor and Tom.

"Nothing really from the phone records. They are focused around Hull, one on the M62 between Hull and Leeds, and one in Leeds. But I've had better luck with the website. Traced the creator to a street in Hull. I reckon if we go there, I could narrow it down to the house."

Luke looked at Connor and said, "I don't know how he does it."

"Magic," said Charlie. "What's that saying you told me, Connor?"

"'Any sufficiently advanced technology is indistinguishable from magic'. An Arthur C Clarke quote."

It amused Connor that Charlie wasn't aware he worked with one of the planet's very best in computer technology. The man behind The Chameleon Project's logistical, technical and intelligence support, the Peruvian-born Jaime Rangel, had been described by various superlatives in that field.

"Exactly," said Charlie. "In a few years' time I'll be like the Gandalf of the computer technology world."

Luke said, "Paul Daniels more like."

"Don't be jealous, Luke. We all have our strengths. Yours is punching people and looking like the Third Reich's fantasy man. And mine is being the bedrock of our family empire's logistical needs."

Connor was unsuccessful at hiding a smirk at Charlie's playful bravado, and he saw Luke had failed too. "You two got much on today?"

Luke shrugged. "I can tell Bill I'm not coming in until later."

His cousin was referring to one of the old and bold who helped Luke manage and co-ordinate the transportation—both legal and illegal—domestically and in Europe.

When Connor looked at Charlie, his younger cousin said, "Nothing that can't be pushed over. Besides, everyone knows the hardest man to come out of Hull is *John Prescott.*"

Connor smiled. "All right, let's take a jolly over. We'll get some breakfast on the way."

Rene took in the view of the lone man sailing against the backdrop of green fields and sparse blue and white clouds above. The light shower had not long petered out.

This was the first time she had walked around Yeadon Tarn, also known as Yeadon Dam, a water feature about three-quarters of a mile in circumference.

Birdsong floated on the breeze.

Paulette stood with her as the white swans, black-necked Brent geese and luxuriant green-headed male Mallard ducks with their brown female companions, fought around them for the vegetable peelings the two widows fed to them.

Finally, Rene leant down to show the gaggle her empty paper bag. "See, all gone."

They eventually got the message and slid back into the water.

"Lovely day, isn't it?"

"Yes," replied Paulette.

An airplane roared close overhead making Rene jump. "Christ, where did that come from?"

"The airport is less than a mile away, you daft bat."

Rene smiled—Paulette's manner could be abrasive and off-putting for some, but Rene doubted she could ever have a better friend.

"I miss walks with him, you know," she said, as they wandered along the path. "Sorry, Paulette."

"What you being sorry for?"

"Being maudlin."

"Don't be silly. I miss Frank every day—daft bugger he was."

"Your grandchildren think the world of you."

"Most grandchildren are fond of their gran."

"How many do you have?"

"Eight. Two girls and six boys."

They walked along a bit further and Rene asked, "That chair. The leather recliner."

"Frank's old chair?"

"Yes. I have noticed when your family or anyone else comes around no one sits in that chair. Even when the sofa's crowded."

"What of it?"

"Well, I don't think they do it just out of respect. Why did you practically kick your grandson, Connor, into it when he visited? Is he your favourite? It's OK to have one."

"It is nothing to do with him being the favourite or not."

"Then what? I don't understand. I am sorry if I'm *mithering* you."

"If you were mithering me, I would let you know about it," said Paulette, before sighing. "You are too smart a woman, Rene, not to have guessed they are not, let's say…'ordinary men', and though I'm not privy to the specifics, what I do know is, when things get really bad, they all look to him. Even my sons do. He is the strongest, in his head, I mean, and the most capable. Thomas is the glue, but even he looks up to Connor, despite being the eldest. That's why he gets to sit in Frank's chair."

Luke sneaked the blue Range Rover onto the M62 and knocked the windscreen wiper settings down now the spray had cleaned it. One of the businesses he had invested in had been a car rental in the city centre. He regularly switched vehicles, as Tom had encouraged him to.

Connor sat in the passenger seat and Charlie in the back.

Luke saw an airplane fly overhead. "Charlie has been educating me on conspiracy theories. What do you think of chemtrails, Connor?"

Connor said, "It's the food they have on airplanes that's trying to kill you."

"You don't eat on flights, Connor?" asked Charlie.

"I would rather guide your dad into his mum than eat airline food."

There was a moment of silence before Charlie said, "You remember my dad—your uncle—was murdered?"

"Exactly," said Connor.

Luke burst out laughing, which slowly caused Charlie to do the same.

Once it had subsided, Connor asked, "What's the education about conspiracies?"

Charlie took out his phone and tapped on it. He showed Connor an inverted pyramid divided into five sections. From the top down the sections were: 'The Antisemitic Point of No Return', 'Science Denial', 'Leaving Reality', 'Speculation', and 'Things that Actually Happened'. Listed underneath each were a host of theories.

"What do you think about that, Connor?" asked Luke, once his older cousin had looked up and handed back the phone.

"I think whoever made that up is very arrogant to think they know everything that has and hasn't happened, let alone present them."

"So, you think the Royal Family could be alien reptile overlords?" exclaimed Charlie.

"Of course not. But lumping that in with the 5G rollout is something that, whoever made it up, is trying to make people feel stupid for questioning certain things. I think 5G is safe, but some respected scientists voice their concerns."

"I know you don't have social media," said Luke. "But some people think they are experts after looking at a few memes and watching a few YouTube videos. I think I'd rather get my information off the experts."

Connor said, "Everyone has innate biases. The trick is to study just as hard against your own argument. Charlie Munger is Warren Buffet's right-hand man, has been for decades, and when he gets an instinct for an investment he'll study hard to disprove himself. The people you're talking about will share something just because the statement fits into their perspective. If they do any study, it's to bolster their own argument—selective conclusion shopping."

Charlie spoke from the back. "Just one on your 'I'll just blindly believe the experts', Luke, is in the sixties doctors prescribed thalidomide to treat morning sickness—which led to defects."

"I get your point," said Luke.

Connor said, "Tell you what that diagram is right about: there're some things that aren't disputed that have happened that are mental."

The voice from the back said, "Any favourites?"

"Loads. One is the Tuskegee Syphilis Study, where the United States Public Health Service—this was between 1932 and 1972—got these poor black guys from Alabama in and promised them free health care to take part in a study. There were six hundred of them in all, with three hundred and ninety-nine latent syphilis—"

"What's latent mean?" asked Luke.

"That the symptoms hadn't manifested yet."

"I see."

"I think the researchers thought, 'Well, we didn't give them the disease and they wouldn't have got treatment anyway', because although penicillin was discovered in 1928, it didn't become widely available until the forties. They could have treated it, but some of the methods available at the time were highly toxic and only mildly effective. The researchers wanted to see what syphilis would do if left untreated, so they—"

"Fuck me," exclaimed Luke. "They could do that?"

"The study was meant to last six months. Naturally, they never told the lads, but when penicillin became widely available in the late forties, they were still never treated."

"How did it stop? They all die?" asked Luke.

Connor shook his head. "Over a hundred of the poor bastards died, either of syphilis or related complications. Forty of the wives got infected. Nineteen of their children were born with congenital syphilis. Apparently, there was a leak to the press and it all came to light. The survivors, along with the heirs of who died, received a ten-million-dollar, out-of-court settlement, and guidelines were introduced to protect people in US government-funded experiments. Bill Clinton made a public apology in 1997. But you see what I mean—and there're loads of things undisputed and equally mental."

Luke's Bluetooth connected phone filled the car with its musical tone.

"It's Tom," said Luke, before answering it.

Tom's voice came through the speakers, "Have you picked up Connor?"

"I'm here, Tom."

"Just you, Luke and Charlie there?"

"Yeh."

"What youse up to?"

Connor replied, "Following a lead. Out East Ridings way."

"Following a lead." Tom laughed. "You the dynamic trio?"

"Yeh," said Connor. "Batman, Robin and Catwoman."

"What lead?"

"Charlie found out the address of the web creator."

"Nice one, Charles," Tom called out. "Listen, I'm here with the new builders—those cowboys left her kitchen looking like something from the Blitz. And one of the cunts has left chewing gum stuck under the stair bannister."

Luke noticed Connor staring straight ahead, expressionless, before he said, "Good to know. I'll come around later and give you a heads-up."

When Tom had gone, Luke said, "Fuckin' rancid, that."

Charlie added, "Just heathens, as Gran would say."

Luke noticed Connor had a big smile. His elder cousin said, almost to himself, "Of all the grannies these bullying daytime-TV-watching rats could have fucked over, it had to be one of our gran's friends. It's like God decided to give us a gift."

6

Callum Jefferies wandered through the quiet and prosperous residential area of Chevening Park with his hands thrust into his green hoodie pockets. In one of his hands, he clutched a polythene-wrapped cannabis resin block the size of a large bar of soap. In the other, a stack of cash.

Despite his appearance being out of kilter with his surroundings, the scraggily haired, seventeen-year-old lived in perhaps the most expensive house in the area.

His father spent most of his time consulting in Dubai, and he and his mum lived comfortably in the house.

He knew his mum would let him get away with murder. And he guessed this was down to her guilt. She had accidentally spilt the contents of a teapot on his face when he was a toddler, which had left one-half disfigured. Hence her never taking him to task over his smoking weed in his room—he opened the window at least. And it had only been on his father's insistence he went to school.

Callum pretty much got anything he wanted, including all the computer equipment, which led him to become a businessman in his own right, selling his skills.

They all paid him a tidy sum, though Paul Troy usually just handed him blocks of weed. They were happy, and he was happy—except when he had to make the half-mile walk to the park to get his supply.

Eventually, he reached his street. Near the top of the hill lay his rustic-red brick house. So big, with two garages and a drive, people often thought it was two houses in one.

The neighbours across the street and a few doors up must have been having visitors, as a dark blue Range Rover with tinted windows was parked outside.

He hoped his mum was out in the kitchen or back garden, as she would only ask him a set of inane questions about why he was back so early. All he wanted to do now was lock his door, get high and celebrate another wad of money by donning his state-of-the-art VR headset and have one of his favourite porn stars take him in hand.

Connor said, "This kid sauntering up the road in the green hoodie with a face like a half-eaten Wine Gum, he's the lad we're looking for."

Luke had parked the Range Rover a mere five minutes ago, as Charlie began to tap on a slim laptop to triangulate the exact house they were looking for.

Luke asked with incredulity, "How do you know that? He's miles away?"

"He's between two hundred and ten and two hundred and twenty metres away. He looks a bit of a digital nerd."

"Why? Because of his face?"

"Why do you think Charlie is deep into computers?"

Luke smirked.

"I am not biting," said the voice from the back. "It's that house there. Number thirty-seven."

"You got a name?"

"Wait…Callum Jefferies. He's the youngest male resident. He's seventeen…that's him, yeh, burnt face."

Luke asked, "Why is he out and about if you're saying he's a hermit? He hasn't got any shopping?"

With Callum Jefferies now being close, Connor's mind whirred—*Why was he out? Coming back from friends? He's come from the park's direction—a bit old to be playing in parks. Unless…*

Connor's hand shot beneath the seat and pulled out his woven satchel. He fired into one of the secret compartments within the stitching. He pulled out his fake Police Identification badge.

"You two stay here. I am going try to get him in the car—without touching him. If I succeed, Charlie, you move into the front seat and Luke, just drive like you know where you are going."

Before they could reply, he alighted from the Range Rover and approached the clearly startled seventeen-year-old.

Putting on his best plain-clothes-copper's voice, Connor began, "Mr Callum Jefferies?"

As the teenager gave a spluttering affirmation, Connor flashed him the identification.

"As of yet, you are not under arrest, we just want a quick chat. Your parents do not need to know and nothing will go on public record. However, if you refuse, we can enact our powers of search. Depending on what is found, an arrest may be forthcoming. Your parents will have to be notified and you will be handcuffed. Do you understand?"

The nodding began slowly, before resembling a woodpecker.

Connor added, "I suggest we make our way to the Range Rover before the neighbours get suspicious."

"Will I…are you…going to search me in there?"

"Believe me, lad, you're not the one we are after."

Jefferies followed him like a fearful dog following its owner through a wolf-infested forest.

The door on the other side clicked open as Charlie walked around the bonnet. Connor opened the back door. Jefferies got in and shuffled over. When Connor got in he could see the unmarked side of the lad's face to be handsome.

The moment Connor's door shut, Luke activated the central locking and started the engine.

"Whe…where we going? Thought it was just a chat."

Connor's hand shot out and bounced the youngster's head off the window. He snatched his hair with one hand and his Adam's apple with the other.

The former marine spat venomously, "It will be just a chat, you snivelling little cunt, as long you never lie or refuse to answer the questions I am about to ask. Every time you do, I am going to break one of your fingers. Now let's begin."

Fred placed the cup of coffee in front of his brother, Andrew, before switching on the ceiling fan and sitting in his leather chair.

They were in Fred's living room, each at a forty-five-degree angle to the giant TV, the dissected screen showing nine images from different areas outside the house.

The older brother said, "Had a call from the gaffer of The Tavern. Says that it's become free for our Nat's welcome home party."

"Good."

Fred took a sip of his coffee and asked, "How come you sent Mark in by himself?"

"No sense two of us being seen by them."

Fred stared at Andrew. "I know he's a fuckhead, but he's still family."

"Exactly. So, this way, he can take the credit. You know how he mopes and wants to impress."

"And so it's him who gets the pinch should they run to the coppers."

Andrew shrugged. "That's just common sense, given how much I bring to the table compared to him. And you might be the one who has a soft spot for him, but it's me who's been havin' to fight his battles for him and sweep up all the messes he's made. Next time, get someone else to look after him."

Fred remained quiet for a moment. A few years ago, Andrew would never have dared speak to him like this in his own house. But he was right, he had been pulling in a lot of money in the last couple of years.

"Don't *mouse*, I just wanted to know."

"I reckon he enjoyed it, anyhow. Should have seen him bounding back up the *ten-foot*, almost skipping he was."

"What did he say he'd done?"

"Gave the bloke a slap. *Brock* one of the dog's hind legs, then throttled her a bit and told her what's what. Job done."

"He brock one of the dogs' legs?" asked Fred, with disgust.

"I didn't ask him to do that."

After a few moments' silence, Fred said, "If they weren't coffin-dodgers to start with, then I reckon that home invasion will have aged 'em."

They both chortled.

"Think they'll run to the coppers?" asked Andrew.

"Nah, too fucking scared to." Fred drained his cup of tea. "There won't be any comebacks from this. See, Mark does have his uses."

"Suppose," said Andrew.

"T'was gonna ask ya. A missing person's report has been filed for Bigga C Thompson," said Fred. "Anything to do with you?"

The younger brother shook his head. "Nah. But plenty will think we have, I reckon. Which is a good thing. The coppers will be sniffing around, but fuck 'em."

"Then what's up with ya? You don't seem yourself?"

His brother paused for a second before shaking his head. "Am all right. Just got a lot on my plate at the moment."

7

Connor pulled the black 1995 Triumph Speed Triple into the car park. After cutting the engine and removing his helmet, he walked over to the scaffolding-caged building.

On a break and sitting on the steps outside, the workers seemed to stiffen on his approach and he noticed one surreptitiously put out his cigarette.

"How you getting on, lads?"

When they all murmured they were fine, he added, "Tell you what, after the day I've had I can't wait to get home and rip my girlfriend's knickers off."

He put his thumb down his belt at the back and said, "Cos they're fucking cutting right into me."

After a moment, they erupted into laughter and visibly relaxed.

He looked to the eldest of the six. "Is Tom in there?"

"Yeh," said the Scotsman with a smile. "He's at the back, talking with our gaffer."

Connor walked into the building undergoing a massive refurbishment. Though the inside was still a skeleton of chrome, polished wood, stainless steel and hanging light fixtures, he could see the layout of the stage, seating, bar and the upstairs VIP area—the protective films obscuring the glass screens. He could smell the vaporised metal from the welder on the stairs.

Tom stood at the far end of the stage in conversation with a suit who Connor presumed to be an architect or chief of the construction team. Tom looked up to greet his eye, and his voice boomed across the cavernous hall, "There's a kettle behind the upstairs bar. Make yourself a coffee. I'll be up in a minute."

"Do you want owt?" Connor shouted back.

"Yeh, a *Julie Andrews*."

"Anyone else, since I am making 'em?"

The workers turned to look at him and chorused, "No, thanks."

Reaching the top of the stairs, Connor could see they had already put in the seating overlooking the downstairs area.

He made the drinks and plonked himself in one of the booths.

Tom joined him and Connor said, "You look vexed?"

His elder cousin sighed. "There is an infestation of rats. It's a fucking nightmare."

"What's Cara said?"

Connor was referring to Tom's girlfriend and manageress of Leeds's most profitable lap dancing club, 'The Dancing Bear'. This would be her and Tom's second joint venture.

"I want to have a solution before I tell, or else she'll constantly be in my earhole about it." Tom smiled. "What have you found out following your lead?"

"The guy's name is Mark Troy. He's a low rank of the—"

"Troy family in Hull."

"Yeh." Connor nodded. Tom's knowledge of criminals of any relevancy in the UK was encyclopaedic.

"Fuck's sake," he murmured.

Connor searched his eyes and asked, "What is it?"

"What do you mean, 'What is it?'? We can't just give him a kicking. There will be reprisals."

"That family is fuck-all in comparison to what we've already seen off. Luke told me they are a set of former rugby players who pump coke, breed dogs, as well as rip off old women."

Tom looked at him. "Andrew Troy has a line on guns and drugs from Holland. With law enforcement keeping their beady eyes on Dover and Folkestone, certain people see Hull as a bit safer and him as a major distributor. The *NCA* might have a Firearms Threat Centre now, but they focus in and around Manchester and Liverpool—something like seventy per cent of the country's guns are there. So, this Andrew Troy is being seen as a 'safer' option. He came to me looking to supply not long back, but I turned him down. But they do steady numbers across the board and now have friends in many cities. What I am trying to say is they are not yokels any more."

"I could kill the main guys by myself without batting an eyelid," said Connor.

"I know you could, but it's not just British crime factions they are in league with. This Andrew Troy has forged friendships with some of the Kosovans in Hull. He'll probably be helping to transport immigrants in for them."

Connor sneered. "Some of them will be slaves, which would have William Wilberforce rolling in his grave."

He was referring to the Hull politician whose twenty-year campaign resulted in abolishing the British slave trade in 1807.

"Some will be, but some will be family members, including young men."

"I don't understand. You looked horrified when I said not to let the family as a whole deal with this. Said we couldn't turn our backs on our roots."

"I've calmed a bit, and that was when we thought it was a couple of scrote builders. With this lot, you'd have to kill at least three, and over what? Them ripping off an old woman? We've sorted her out a kitchen that exceeds what she paid them for, anyway."

For the first time in years, Connor couldn't believe or understand the logic behind his cousin's words.

"There's something else at play. Just tell me."

Tom sighed. "We have a sort of unspoken arrangement with the local police. If our family keep a lid on things, smooth out any tensions between gangs, make sure crackhead zombies aren't robbing people left, right and Chelsea, and little rats aren't running around with guns, they'll turn a blind eye to certain things."

"Very specific for an unspoken agreement."

"Well, it was spoken, but informally. And I've been running our business long enough to know they are holding up their end of the bargain. It's a cushty deal if we can maintain it—cos usually, for an organisation to get something like this off the local police, it's because they're having to pay or turn grass."

"So, what's the issue?"

"There has been a spate of guns—Harehills, Seacroft and Chapeltown. No shootings yet, but I

55

don't know where the fuck they are coming from. I've put the word out but there's nothing."

"How have you put the word out?"

"I've thrown our Curtis a bone, and he's looking into it. If he can ID them, then I can give him a pat on the back and it'll stop him being a sulking bastard," said Tom, before taking a sip of his coffee. "But we need to get this weighed off, or they start putting heavy pressure on us."

Connor nodded. "Then what are you saying? We do nothing until this is sorted?"

"No, not nothing. We'll go over and tax them."

"And this Mark Troy will still continue to do what he's doing."

Tom shrugged. "But he won't be doing it in Leeds."

"That's not the point."

"It is the point. What you going do? Watch re-runs of *Rogue Traders* and find out the addresses of all the dodgy tradesmen on it?"

Momentarily silenced by his cousin's logic, his mind whirred. He felt like a child unwrapping a fantastic gift on Christmas Day only to have it taken away before he could get it out of the box.

"This can't be the way to just let him off. He'll just rob other old ladies to recoup it."

"Look, you know I would never tell you what to do. But you know we're on the rise and have to pick our battles. You're the smartest guy I know, way smarter than me, but we both know if you took a step back from wanting to hurt the guy, you'll realise it's not the best way to deal with it."

"What if he catches a beating but doesn't know where it's come from?"

"What would be the point in that? When he recovers, he'll go back to ripping off old people. At least this way he keeps out of Leeds."

Connor looked at his cousin. "If I can make sure it doesn't come back to us. Would you let me handle it?"

Tom met his eye. "Like I said, I'll never pretend I can tell you what to do."

Under the dark night sky, Andrew Troy watched the seawater-stained shipping container being cranked open. The various wind turbine components hid the treasure.

Ordinarily, he would not put himself at the scene of the crime, but this was only the fourth run with his new Dutch partners and they had requested him to be there until a level of trust had been built.

If all went well, he'd be a multi-millionaire in a few years. Ten million tonnes of cargo went through the Port of Hull each year, which made looking for contraband without reliable tip-offs a nightmare. Not that he had found bribing the security apparatus difficult.

Indeed, the man to his left stood high up in the port's security chain and had opened the container like a member of the monarchy would unveil a new tourist attraction.

This time it was guns and drugs, but in the months to come it would be more immigrants on behalf of Hektor Dekovi. Troy had originally courted them, knowing immigrants not on record, with the ability to slink back into their communities or even return home, could be useful. And he had kept the nature of the relationship from Fred.

However, he now felt the balance of power between him and the Serbs shifting in a scary way. The way Bigga C's sliced-off face stuck to the mannequin head reminded him of Hannibal Lecter's escape in *The Silence of the Lambs*.

"Do you want to check before…you know?" asked the portly officer, nervously.

Andrew shook his head. "Your job was to see I had proper access to my container. The lads and I will take it from here."

With that, he delved into his jacket pocket and handed the officer a bulging envelope full of fifty-pound notes.

"How long do you need?"

"Giz twenty minutes."

The officer wandered off. Troy stepped into the container, found the package marked with blue tape in the shape of a cross and tucked it under his arm. Upon exiting he said to the two men on his right, "Right, gloves on. Grab your copies of your lists. If you leave anything on those lists in here, I'll cut yer fingers off. Load your trucks and meet the suppliers tomorrow night at the agreed location. Make sure the right packages go to the right people. I won't be there, so you better be on top of this. You pair understand?"

They nodded in unison.

"Any questions?"

They shook their heads, and Andrew left them to it.

Rene alighted from the car's passenger seat and waited for Paulette to join her on the pavement. Tom got out of the car parked behind and converged on her just as Paulette did.

He handed her back her house keys and said, "I'll come in with you, Rene, in case there is anything you're not happy with."

"I am sure it'll be grand," she replied, knowing she would put on a performance worthy of Meryl Streep even if it wasn't.

"Come on then," said Paulette. "No use in hanging around like hobos on the street."

They entered the house and made for the kitchen.

She gasped on entry; it was better than she could have ever envisioned.

The white marble countertops had featherings of blue smudged through them, giving her the mind of clouds. The turquoise muffin stools surrounded a central table covered with the same marble as the countertops. Smooth brickwork made up one side of her kitchen with recesses for housing her cooker and kitchen utensils. The floral-patterned lampshades threw amber tones, and the bay windows let in her garden's greenery.

She felt the moisture creep underneath her eyelids.

"I don't know what to say. I just wanted a bit of a freshen-up—this is amazing. You have to let me pay you."

"Don't be silly. We recovered your money off the original builders," lied Tom. Though he planned to, there was no point making the old dear feel guilty. "We didn't think you'd want them back in, so we hired better blokes."

59

"But…but this amount of work must have cost more than—"

"Do you not clean your *lugholes*, Rene?" exclaimed Paulette. "He doesn't need any money. Just say thank you."

Rene, though her offer of payment was sincere, knew it would never be accepted. She turned to Tom and said, "Thank you very much. You've made an old woman very happy."

"Well," he replied. "Any lady who can put up with two weeks with my gran deserves a kitchen like this."

Rene noticed Paulette staring at him, and Tom said, "Just joking, Gran."

"Now then, Rene," said Paulette. "We will leave you to it."

An unexpected hit of melancholy plumed within Rene's stomach at the words. As Paulette put an awkward hand on her shoulder before departing, Rene understood why she felt like this.

She had enjoyed her near two-week stay with Paulette—more than she thought she would. She was not particularly looking forward to nights in on her own again.

As if sensing how upset she was getting, her phone began to vibrate in her pocket. Her surroundings brightened when she saw it was her granddaughter.

"Hiya, lovely. How's your trip to Ireland?"

8

From his car, Andrew looked out into the darkness of the truck depot in Selby. He had reclined his seat back so as not to silhouette his head.

He was parked well over a hundred metres away from the designated spot where the port's cargo would be distributed.

Being in Selby was ideal, as it did not lie far away from the M1 motorway connecting Leeds to London and fed into some of the UK's major cities along the way.

One of his paid contacts had demonstrated to him the massive blind spot in the depot's security camera coverage, and as long as his lads went to the exact place he had stipulated, they would be fine.

However, he had known since childhood the perils of blindly trusting people. This far back, in the dark, they wouldn't see him. Indeed, if someone came over to give the vehicle a cursory inspection he would be pleased but surprised.

He glanced at the green glow of the illuminated clock—*it's time. Where the fuck are they?*

His temper was only given two minutes to bubble before his vans pulled in. He calmed himself; two minutes was acceptable—just.

Some of the packages contained heroin and had been snapped up by a single dealer distributing in the town of Goole, around thirty miles from Hull. Despite the place having only two per cent of East Riding's population, it had around twelve per cent of the region's heroin users.

It would be this area which Troy would encourage Hektor to take over. Though he fully expected the Serb and his crew to succeed, hopefully the ruthless competition in the area would slow them.

The four customers, in their cars now pulling in, were from other areas of the north. One from Liverpool, one from Manchester, another from Sheffield and finally the last one from Leeds—*little bastard lives the closest, and he's the one that's late. I'll cut him off. He's not worth the potential aggro.*

They were buying low-calibre, untraceable Glocks which he had bought for £136 each. He had imported from China the plastic switches needed to reconvert them into lethal weapons, costing just £3.50 apiece, before selling each converted gun for £5,000. Even after all the expenses included in the transport, reconversion and various bribes, it still made him a killing.

The exchanges took a few minutes, with the buyers going through the requisite checks of the firearms; cocking them, ensuring the firing mechanisms and safety catches worked. In addition to the Glocks, there were a few Baikal handguns modified to fire gas canisters before being turned back into lethal weapons. With the magazine only capable of holding eight rounds, the old-style Eastern European design might not have been in vogue with the posing crowd, but remained popular with 'walk-up-behind-and-shoot-them-in-the-spine' assassins of the underworld due to its compactness.

As he observed events unfold, he could see that not only had he provided the service of supplying firearms, but he might have brought contacts together too.

He remembered a term, 'The Yellow pages of Crime', used by a 'celebrity gangster', and wondered if it was a good thing or not.

The Liverpool, Manchester and Sheffield buyers left, leaving his men and the Leeds buyer.

What's this prat fucking around for? Just check the guns and fuck off.

Andrew's irritability began to scorch into a rage that placed his hand to open the door. Just as his discipline burnt away, a black van zoomed into the truck depot, rocketing his heart rate in dread.

However, it was not the police who had just arrived. Even from this distance, he could make out Hektor Dekovi alighting from the van after his men had.

Connor looked across the mat and kept his face expressionless, despite being aware of his opponent's desire to 'destroy' him in this session of grappling.

He had opted to hotel in Hull for the next couple of weeks, to conduct a reconnaissance mission on Mark Troy.

Arriving the previous evening, and with car crime on the up in Hull, he had booked out a secure but nondescript grey Skoda Fabia. He had decided to treat it as more of an exploration with the surveillance thrown in. As much as it pained him, he knew his older cousin was correct; a beating would only make himself feel better and nothing else. And, if Connor did tell him what it was for, he would invite a war for a reason that didn't warrant the danger or financial resources—*sometimes you have to pick your battles.*

Connor knew the reason he was here; it was in the hope that in tracking Mark Troy he would discover him to be a heinous monster, and thus it would become his moral duty to put him out of action.

Still, there was plenty of time for that, so Connor had opted to attend a NoGi submission wrestling session at one of the respected MMA clubs in the city.

The former Western and Thai-boxer didn't like referring to grappling matches as 'fights', as the threat of being knocked out was removed. He had heard it said that the submission was the grappling equivalent of the knockout, and only a no-holds-barred street altercation could be considered a true 'fight'. Connor was not convinced, as for him, though to issue a tap of submission would leave him smarting from embarrassment, he imagined it would pale in comparison to actually being knocked out—something he had yet to endure.

Still, he had made the recent decision to limit his exposure to being struck—not due to the fear of being knocked out or hurt, but of being brain-damaged, if he wasn't to some degree already. Now nearing thirty years old, he was aware striking effectively required sharp reflexes. He still possessed them, but knew he wouldn't forever—especially without their constant honing. He had read a few studies showing MMA fighters five years into their careers did not show a great deal of brain damage as a general rule. However, ten-year veterans showed significant damage. Connor had long ago exceeded the five-year mark, in both a civilian and military boxing career, along with many Thai-boxing matches, MMA sparring sessions and numerous street altercations. He now limited his striking sparring sessions, and instead focused on keeping his 'hitting muscles' strong on the heavy bag.

The class tonight was concentrating on the *ADCC* ruleset which, unlike most Brazilian jiu-jitsu competitions, discouraged the practice of *'pulling guard'*. The onus was to wrestle your opponent down from the standing position. His shoulder, stiff initially, had not bothered him once warm, and neither had his shrapnel marks.

His shorn-haired opponent, covered in a multitude of tattoos, stood bare from the waist up across from him. Connor estimated him to be around the same weight, a little taller and broader.

The timer sounded and after a bump of fists, they circled one another.

The Leeds man threw a palm at face level to disguise his double-leg takedown feint. When his opponent sprawled his legs back in defence, Connor snatched him into a front headlock and drove his face into the mat. The man's quick reactions in thrusting his hands out prevented a broken nose, but left him vulnerable to the guillotine choke the former marine rifled in.

He briefly considered letting his opponent escape, given the sequence's rapidity in front of his club mates. Connor admonished himself—*Don't patronise the lad.*

He felt the tap and immediately released him.

His rival wrestled him hard for the remainder of the round, but Connor sensed an underlying caginess against being submitted again, which prevented his partner from fully committing.

He went through the rest of the class, outwrestling most, submitting a few before finding himself in a leg entanglement he could not extract from in time, and tapping to a heel hook.

He scolded himself—*You get caught in them more than anything else. When you going to take the fucking hint?*

Still, he thanked the victor for the lesson before using the foam roller in the informal and communal warm-down.

The man who had submitted him, the same height as Connor, with a thick black beard perfectly matching the length and colour of his hair, sat across from him and asked, "Where are you from, then?"

"Leeds."

"I thought you were Wezzy, accent isn't tha' strong though. You a staying here or a *comfer*?"

"Just a comfer. It's to discuss business contracts. You might know him. His name is Mark Troy. Apparently, his family are renowned around here?"

He saw the guy's face drop. Connor, feeling a flutter, said encouragingly, "Go on, tell me."

"Tell you what?"

"Listen, I don't know your name and you don't know mine. Whatever you tell me is going to stay between us. I just need to know who I am getting into bed with."

The man's cheeks billowed out and he said, "Well, I am sure you're aware of him and his family's reputation?"

"Yeh, I've got the internet."

The man frowned. "You're not a copper, are you?"

Connor broke into a grin. "No, mate. I am not a copper."

"All right then. Well, they are all bad news, but this Mark Troy has taken to ripping off old people and the disabled. A few weeks back, he left this blind Korean war veteran without a bathroom. But the latest one is horrendous."

"Am listening."

"His sister and her fella are getting out of prison soon, big scam on social media to do with online buying. Anyway, the family decided they wanted a big party to celebrate their release. The only problem was this old couple had already booked the function room for their granddaughter's graduation."

"So, they leaned on the bar's owner to cancel?"

"Nah, mate," said the grappler, solemnly. "If the bar owner cancelled then it would have brought bad press on it. And the Troys couldn't be having that; they tax the place. Not that it's common knowledge."

"How do you know all this?" asked Connor, before catching the guy's expression, and repeating, "I am not a copper, Scout's honour."

"I have like far-off links to them."

"Tenuous links."

"Yeh, that's the word—tenuous."

"So, what happened?" Connor began to stretch off his shoulders.

"They sent this Mark, big fat fucker he is, around this granny and grandad's home. He bursts in. Knocks the old boy out. Grips the old gal by the throat and tells her to cancel the graduation party."

"He sounds like a lovely man."

The grappler exchanged 'byes' with a few departing members before turning his attention back to Connor.

"It wasn't just that. They had a couple of Yorkshire terriers. Mark Troy snapped one of the poor bastard's hind legs. Said he'd do worse if they went to the police or refused to cancel the party."

Connor's stomach lurched with revulsion and hate.

The man continued, "Sorry if that's ruined any big plans."

The black operations agent shook his head, and felt a smile threatening to creep to his mouth. "Nah, mate, that's exactly what I needed to hear."

Tom stood with the lead builder within the club refurbishment.

"These rats haven't magically disappeared then?" he asked, rhetorically.

"Afraid not. When it's quiet you can hear 'em. Seems to be more. Can seal where they are getting in, but it's the ones already in here that's the problem," said the gruff Scotsman.

"Someone is arriving shortly to sort it," answered Tom.

As if he hadn't heard him, the builder continued, "The problem we have is this. If you put traps down it'll catch some of the adult rats but the younger ones will still be about. Poison is usually the best, as the parent rats take it back and poison their own *weans*, but the smell will be horrid for a while. In the seventies, on the shipyards, we used 'worker cats' to kill 'em. Docked their tails, so we did, and any cats wandering around with a tail would be known as a tourist."

The Scotsman laughed, patting the smiling Tom in his torso with the back of his hand, before continuing, "But even the cats are soft nowadays, they'd just play with them. So what you ne—"

The echoing bellow made the Scotsman jump.

"Now then, Thomas! How's me favourite *Gorga*?"

Hughie Birtle stood at the entrance surveying the scene before him.

As large as life as ever—thought Tom.

The big Romany gypsy wore his usual braces over chequered red and white shirt; the rolled-up sleeves revealed tanned forearms finishing at bulbous knuckles. His slicked-back, feathered black hair framed a clean-shaven but weathered face.

"Very well, Hughie. Would you and your lads like a brew?" asked Tom.

He sauntered further in with a group of his relatives. Three were pulling back on the leads of terriers straining against them. From the hands of the other three dangled cages, holding evil-looking and animated ferrets.

"No, thank you, Thomas," answered Birtle, in his usual slightly-louder-than-necessary voice. "It's cruel to keep God's creatures restrained when they are going wild to fetch vermin. Empty the room and lock those doors."

Within a minute, the building crew were gone, leaving only Tom and the gypsies in the locked buildings.

The ferrets and terriers were released. The sounds of animal genocide soon rose up around them.

The ferrets darted into holes, nooks and crannies Tom hadn't even known were there. The desperate rats began to appear from nowhere only to be snatched up by terriers and violently ragged to death.

Birtle's lads shouted encouragement and praise to their furred companions.

Hughie, standing next to Tom said, "Look how happy those terriers and ferrets are. We take an instinct, train it, and this is the result—a beautiful massacre of unwelcome guests."

Akhtar Karrar sat in his new model blue Subaru Impreza with two of his cousins in the back. Set back into the treeline overlooking the dirt path leading to rural Harewood Park of Leeds, they waited for their gun supplier to arrive.

This would be Karrar's fourth run with his new young partner, and the volume had increased. Karrar, from the town of Halifax around twenty-five miles away, had been quietly supplying lads from Huddersfield, Oldham and Rotherham. He planned on becoming the 'go-to' man for weapons, to rule the Calderdale region encompassing Halifax and the surrounding areas. After that, he and his crew would be seen as equal to any of the Bradford gangs.

Not for the first time, the contact was running late.

His cousin Talib spoke from the back. "Where the fuck is this Gora?"

He used the Punjabi term meaning white person.

Before Akhtar could answer a black van appeared.

Furqaan, in the driver's seat, barked, "Who the fuck is that? *Pulisa?*"

Akhtar caught sight of his contact's face, and placed a calming hand on his older cousin's arm, stopping him from starting the car.

"It's him. Calm your'sen."

Talib growled, "Who the fuck 'as he brought with him? His family?"

"I don't think so," said Akhtar, watching two other men get out. "Not the main boys at least, I'd recognise 'em. Let's get this over with."

They all alighted from the Impreza, and Akhtar exclaimed, "What the fuck? We didn't agree to any strangers."

The Leeds man said, "These are my associates. They wanted to meet you cos am getting spread thin."

The smaller but stocky middle-aged man stared with the whites of his eyes showing. The younger, taller one stood back, looking over Akhtar's shoulder at his cousin.

Akhtar tilted his chin towards the smaller man and said, "Do they speak? Or they just here to stand and act hard?"

His contact's reply was cut off by the man's strangely accented voice. "You Indian?"

"Nah. Am a Pakistani-British. What are you? Polish?"

"Muslim?"

"Well, I aren't going to be a fuckin' brown Christian from Gibbet Street, Halifax, am I?" answered Akhtar with disdained amusement. His cousins joined him in laughing.

Then Akhtar clapped his hands. "Where are they then? Chop fuckin' chop. They better work like the others an'all."

71

The two strangers went over to the van, opened the slider door and leant inside.

Akhtar's legs emptied as they walked back with the Glocks in hands.

The bulky one said, "Guns work good. I not like Muslims."

Sledgehammers punctured Akhtar's body as the bangs hammered his eardrums.

And then, nothing.

9

Tom drove through the Horsforth as the sun began to rise over the civil parish of Leeds.

Sat beside him, Luke asked, "Any ideas what they want?"

Tom shook his head. "Them requesting to meet isn't a good sign in the first place. Them calling that late last night, leaving a voicemail to meet this early isn't good at all."

Luke asked, "How does he contact you?"

"I have a separate phone I check in with," said Tom. "I presume he has too. When we get back, I'll show you where I keep it."

"I see," said Luke. "Aren't they going to be fucked off you're bringing me?"

Tom shrugged. "I'll hide you around the corner and give them the heads-up. They can only say 'no'."

He turned into Scotland Lane, rural but with intermittent houses on either side, and parked a short way down.

"It's around the back of house that's being renovated. Let's go."

After a two-minute walk, Tom cut them both across the road to an isolated house caged in scaffolding.

They entered the gate with a low clang.

Tom turned to his younger cousin. "Wait here until if and when I call you around."

Luke nodded.

The Ryder family leader rounded the corner to be confronted by two men, one he knew and one he didn't.

Though backchannel communications between the Ryder family and local law enforcement went back nearly two decades, the faces—on both sides—had changed for these meetings a few times. This was due to the freedom of movement of a police officer becoming restricted as he ascended rank, and they usually passed the baton once they had obtained the level of DCI (Detective Chief Inspector).

However, Tom had known Arthur Berry of the local CID (Criminal Investigation Department), back when the Policeman was Detective Constable several years ago.

Berry was now a DI (Detective Inspector) within the *HMET* unit. Tom, through other contacts, knew Berry liaised with the Yorkshire and Humber regional organised crime unit named ODYSSEY that supported the NCA.

Around a similar age to Tom, Arthur stood four inches taller at six-feet. He sported a heavy black beard matching his hair in colour and thickness. The short-hemmed tweed jacket wrapped around his beige cord trousers.

"Thomas, thank you for meeting me at short notice," said Arthur.

The Leeds gangster noted the unusual formality in his voice. Whether it was to do with the gravity of the meeting's purpose or his companion's presence, he could not be sure.

Tom simply nodded, and Arthur introduced the man on his left.

"Tom, this is a colleague of mine."

He didn't give his name—thought Tom.

The man stood between Tom and Arthur in height and looked nearer forty. Around fourteen stone with a tightness in the shoulders, the cropped-haired man reminded Tom of a bulldog.

"Good to meet you," said Tom, before turning to Arthur. "My cousin is around the front. I've brought him so you know who to liaise with should anything happen to me."

There were a few moments of silence, and Arthur asked, "Which one?"

"Luke."

"Luke?" Arthur frowned.

"Yes, Luke," said Tom. "I left him around the corner to give you the respect of asking first."

The DI gave him a tight smile of apology, before turning to the other man who shrugged.

"All right, Tom. Bring him around."

When Luke joined him a few seconds after being called, Tom asked Arthur, "What's up?"

"You were told weeks ago guns were coming into Leeds."

Not liking the tone but understanding it was due to whoever the man next to him was, Tom replied, "No, you said being sold to outsiders in Leeds—not coming in."

Arthur acknowledged this with a nod. "Well, the worst has happened now. Three Asian men have been shot dead up on Harewood Park. We've identified them as low-level players out of Halifax. Thankfully, the police got there before anyone with a smartphone did. Still, this could be highly flammable once the media puts it out, if they haven't already while we've been speaking."

Tom asked, "Any leads?"

"Probably a gangland execution carried out by elements from Bradford."

Tom knew this was code for *'we are going to insinuate it was an Asian-on-Asian hit for damage control.'*

Tom replied, "And this man beside you is going to tell me who you really think is behind it."

The Bulldog replied, "He said you were smart."

"Time will tell."

"That it will," the man replied. "A card found in one of the victim's hands."

With that he stepped forward and revealed his phone. The screen showed a hand clutching a card with a cross. The cross centre appeared to be the letters IC on one arm and XC on the other, facing out at each corner.

The Bulldog continued, "It is a Serbian Orthodox cross."

"OK."

"It's not OK. Back in the Kosovan War, a young teenager named Dušan Dragojević was part of the Serbian paramilitary forces. His unit allegedly committed numerous acts to force Muslims to flee from Kosovo. Then he entered the Serbian mafia, rising through their ranks until an internal conflict led to his expulsion. He seems to have a burning hatred of Muslims, and that card has been linked to him."

"So he's in Leeds?"

The Bulldog said, "We don't know. Interpol reports suggest he was heading to either London or Southampton under the alias of Hektor Dekovi. But there has been neither sight nor sound of him. If you find out, then bring it to Arthur so we can make arrests."

Tom straightened and locked eyes on the man. "I think the nature of this relationship has been misreported to you. We aren't fucking informants—

or covert human intelligence sources, whatever you're calling them now. The Ryder family have been helping to simmer tensions in this city for nearly twenty years, which has helped its resurgence in economic development and is why you rarely see the city in the national news. We don't take money."

"But you do get protected."

"Is this you threatening me?"

The Bulldog matched Tom's posture and tone. "If you knew who I was, you'd know I don't have to."

"I know who you are. You'll be some kind of high-flyer within the NCA, hence the cloak and dagger. Now don't cut your nose off to spite your face—if I come across this guy, it won't end well for him. But it won't be in the form of me grassing on his whereabouts and him being arrested."

It surprised Tom to see the guy's face soften. "This Dušan Dragojević is a very dangerous man. Not only that, the atrocities he committed back in Kosovo included the rape of women with sticks until they bled out, and getting children as young as eight to play Russian Roulette until conclusion."

The Bulldog tapped on his phone's screen before showing it to the cousins. Grisly images appeared, making Tom's stomach lurch and Luke recoil. The elder Ryder nodded.

"I understand. I'll put the word out and if he comes within our orbit, you won't have to worry about him."

"Our intelligence suggests it is doubtful he will remain up here—he's probably back down south. But if you become aware of his presence here then maybe your other cousin Connor Reed will need to be aware of what kind of man this Serb is."

With that, the man gestured to Arthur Berry and the two law enforcement officers left. Once they were out of earshot, Luke's exclamation matched his own thoughts.

"Holy fuck. Did that mean what I think that meant?"

Connor sat in his hired car parked across from a block of high-rise tenement flats on Albany Road.

He turned down the podcast that blared back through the speakers at the termination of his call with Tom.

His cousin said more than once during the call it would be unlikely this Dušan Dragojević character would be hiding in Leeds. If he was just hiding then maybe, but if an outsider was making moves then Tom's network throughout the city would have picked up on it.

Still, Connor wished it was true when Tom described hideous acts the Serb had allegedly committed. Charlie had scoured the dark web and had come to the opinion there was no smoke without fire. The Chameleon Project agent thought of how much he would have loved to capture a man like that.

The inference an NCA representative had—in front of their regular HMET unit contact—given Connor a *Beckett's Approval* disturbed him.

How would they know I'd be capable of that?

He decided to compartmentalise it until after he had solved his immediate challenge of Mark Troy, or when it became relevant.

Now waiting for his prey, Connor knew he would have to curb his desire to hurt the Hull criminal on sight.

From his hired car, he watched Troy come out of a block of high-rise tenement block and stroll across to his black Audi Q5.

Fucking paid for out of old women's pensions.

Though Connor had access to the world's best trackers through his remit as an agent with The Chameleon Project, he could not use them for things like this. While Bruce McQuillan, the head of the black operations group, had encouraged him to increase his standing as a criminal, he had also specified he could not use any of the Project's resources to achieve that aim outside of operations.

However, Charlie had become ultra-adept at sourcing things of that nature through the dark web while minimising the risk of being traced. Unlike the ones he had used on operations, this particular tracker needed to be placed correctly and required a degree of fitting.

Connor began to follow the Audi Q5, keeping two vehicles back as they hit the B-road. He assumed Mark, like many in UK crime organisations, had some form of security apparatus around his home.

He just needed a bit of discretion and time, then he wouldn't have to follow the cretin everywhere around Hull.

When his mind drifted back to his conversation with Tom, Connor decided to call a friend of his.

10

Tom sat in the familiarity of his garage office. After the disturbing call ended, he put the phone down and looked at the raven-haired Miss July on the topless girlie calendar. The mechanic lamented how rare it was to see them nowadays. When he was a youth, the 'lad mag' culture was still popular, with topless models like Lucy Pinder and Michelle Marsh instantly recognisable to the British working man. Nowadays, those sorts of girls were plastered over Instagram to hook clients into their 'Only Fans' subscription pages. Indeed, his girlfriend, Cara, had been a quasi-Instagram sensation before they had met.

Despite the relative glamour of the lap dancing club, it was not really Tom's scene. Luke loved it, and so did Connor, despite being more subtle about it. Instead, Tom had always had a fascination with car mechanics. He often wondered if he would have been happier if he had never become embroiled in the family's nefarious activities and simply run this garage.

A lot less wealthy or powerful, maybe, but he might not have had to deal with problems arising from other family members he presided over. Or issues like the voice on the phone had just informed him of.

He heard the creak of the side door opening next to the main roller doors, and he craned his neck to see Curtis enter. He stood as his cousin bounded up the stairs to greet him.

They shared a hand-clasp-embrace and Tom said, "Put the kettle on. I'll have a tea."

He caught a look on Curtis's face before he quickly complied. A few minutes later they both had a cup of tea in their hands, Curtis a plain cup and himself a Leeds United mug with the slogan, 'Elland Road LS11', and 'Ryder' underneath.

He looked at Curtis with a feeling of hope cooling his exasperation. His second to youngest—by eight minutes—cousin had always had a bolshie attitude as a youth, but it had evolved into a sinister insolence on recent occasions. And Tom knew that Curtis knew that, barring Curtis hurting another family member, he would not raise his hand to his wayward cousin.

"You got anything for me?"

Tom's heart plummeted as Curtis shook his head. "No one seems to know who has them, or where they are coming from, or who was responsible for the shooting of those 'fax lads."

"If we don't find the distributer soon, this family will be in deep shit."

"What do you want me to do? Invade Chapeltown?" exclaimed Curtis, in a voice edged with arrogance.

Tom sharpened his tone, "If that's what it's going to take. We can't have shootings and a flood of guns into this city. I'll be making calls. Luke is down south handling something sensitive but am going to have to cancel it and bring him back up here. I'll put him on this with you and—"

"No, no, no, don't cancel anything cos of this," said Curtis with a sudden contriteness. "I'll handle it. Just give me a few days, please."

Tom looked at him, desperate to give him a chance, and said, "You have two days, then I'll be passing it onto Luke and some of the lads."

Curtis nodded. "All right, I am on it."

Connor walked out of the hardware store on the outskirts of Hull city centre with his purchase tucked under his arm. Although his procurement was not illegal in itself, what he would be using them for would be. To that end, he had worn a baseball cap, angled his head away from the cameras and paid in cash.

He had been thinking about how he would go about tackling the issue. He needed to get Mark Troy alone. But that was difficult, as he lived with his junkie girlfriend. He'd need to get him isolated or at least somewhere quiet for what he was to put him through.

And he had to remain unidentified. He decided to head to Hull's Old Town to have a meal and a drink in the quaint Ye Olde White Harte pub.

He had read that in that pub, in a room now known as the Plotting Parlour, the decision was reputedly taken in 1642 to refuse Charles I entry to the town.

And this led to the English Civil War.

He crossed the road to the car park and got back into his car. No sooner had he hooked his phone up to the car's internal system than it rang.

He answered with, "Yep?"

"It's me. Our dark friend said you had a question for me."

Connor knew Arben Tinaj's reference to his friend Louis Allen as 'our dark friend' was designed to get a rise out of him. Louis was Connor's friend, and had been for years ever since they had met as young soldiers in the Royal Marines. The three-quarter Nigerian, quarter-Irish Londoner now presided over one of the capital's most profitable organised crime groups, the Southwark Union Gang—or SUG for short. Arben Tinaj ruled over the Albanian-centric equivalent Hellbanianz.

Instead he answered, "This a secure line?"

"What do you take me for?"

Connor didn't take the sharp tone personally—their relationship was an uneasy one.

"Serbs—especially the kind that might have raped and murdered Albanian civvies during the Kosovan War—how do you feel about them?"

"The same Kosovan War where NATO bombed the fuck out of it all? Governments just get Chiefs to pull triggers on their big, bad guns no matter where they are pointed."

Connor, knowing 'Chief' meant an unintelligent person in south London slang, and it was a barb at his own military service, said with derision, "That was in defence of your people. That is, if they are still your people."

The Yorkshireman could almost see the British-Albanian smirk at his biting.

"Don't get vexed. Just saying being a fighter pilot these days isn't exactly *Top Gun* now, is it?"

"Look, you didn't answer my question."

"There're not exactly going be on many Albanian Christmas card lists, are they?"

"What about our friend back in the old country?"

Connor was referring to Andrei Faja, the most influential *Kyre*—Boss—in the Mafia Shqiptare, the true Albanian mafia.

"I would think his feelings about them sort of people would be stronger than mine. 'Specially how it all happened closer to his ends."

Luke walked into Lambert Transport Ltd. Various health and safety notices were pinned to the green maize board running the length of the corridor. He could hear the muffled shouts of drivers and depot works through the wall, the clanking of containers being loaded or unloaded and engines starting.

He peered over the reception desk and called out, "Hi, Lynn, you all right?"

The middle-aged brunette looked up from her office desk with a smile. "I am, thanks, luv. Yourself?"

"Yeh, am all right," he answered. "Bill out in the yard?"

"He's out back having a cigarette, luv."

As Luke walked into the office, Lynn asked, "Kettle is boiled. You want a cuppa?"

"Tea, none, please, Lynn."

He didn't particularly want one, and knew the kettle hadn't just boiled, but he understood Lynn had a soft spot for him and it would make her happy.

"I'll come back in for it, Lynn, after I've spoke to Bill."

"All right, luv."

Luke made his way out of the exit door at the back of the office. He skirted the building to his left for around thirty metres before rounding the corner.

He found the sixty-three-year-old Bill Hopkins sat on grey plastic looking out to the distant traffic zipping by on the M621 motorway.

The way Bill smoked almost made Luke want to try it—deep slow draws followed by long exhalations.

Though not a big man, the grooves of his forearms stood out from the black company short-sleeved shirt. Curving around the right wrist were the tattooed words: 'Marching On Together'—the anthem of his beloved Leeds United Football Club.

The black and grey work trousers matched the colours of his cropped hair and goatee.

Luke said, "Staying strong with those cigarettes, Bill. You never thought about vaping?"

Bill looked at him. "Ppffftt. Young'uns don't smoke for pleasure or to reset them'sens—they're just robotic niccy slaves."

Luke smiled and though he remembered Connor talking about mental dissonance, he knew Bill genuinely did not want to stop.

"I'd say thanks for holding the fort but everyone knows you run the place."

"And I get paid loads to do so. Your family 'as always seen me right—well, before and after yer Uncle Derek tried running the place into the ground."

"You get paid whatever you get paid because our Tom says you're excellent and can be trusted. It's not like we're doing you a favour, Bill," said Luke, quickly changing the subject before the older man could interject. "I was going to ask you, is it true you don't have anything red in the house? That you have a blue Santa Claus outfit."

Bill took a draw and smiled. "I wouldn't have anything that reminds me of scum, lad. And neither should you if you're a fan."

Red was the colour of Leeds United's old-time rivals Manchester United.

"No offence, Bill, but I don't think they have been proper rivals since the seventies," said Luke, referring to Manchester United's success in the Premier League in comparison to Leeds's inconsistency over the past few decades. "Though we'll be challenging them now we're back in the Premiership."

"Fuckin' A we'll be challenging. And it's not just to do with football by the way; this goes back to the War of the Roses, that does."

Though Bill never spoke about it, Luke knew he had been a notorious figure within seventies' football hooliganism culture as a teenaged member of the Leeds United Service Crew. And the clashes between that crew and Man United's Red Army were frequent and violent.

"How's things?"

"Bored as a midget in a theme park at the moment, always am pre-season. Off on holiday soon though," said Bill. "Tom told me some fucking bastard ripped yer gran's friend off for a kitchen?"

"Yeh, it's getting sorted."

"Tom didn't say much on the phone but says they are down the road like."

If this conversation had been a year or so ago, Luke would have told Bill everything—*why keep things like this away from a guy who helped you import and export illegal drugs worth millions?* However, Tom and Connor's insistence on 'need to know' had finally taken root.

Still, Bill had been connected with the family since Luke's Grandad Frank's day.

"The person in question isn't heavy himself but his family is. We have to tread carefully."

Luke looked over his shoulder as he thought he heard a sound, but when no one came around the corner he said, "Connor might handle it so it doesn't come back on the family. Like I said, the guy is a mong but needs a lesson."

"What do you think young Connor will do?"

"Well, Tom's asked him not to go too far, so maybe he'll break legs or something. We'll see."

Luke heard a crunching sound behind him again, but as he turned to investigate, he spotted a black cat with matted fur skid from the corner.

Bill said, "Frank told me that boy switched when he was around seven years old from being a sweet-natured sensitive boy to a lad who could turn into a vicious fuckin' animal who'd fight bullies at a drop of a hat. Could be quite cruel, from what I heard."

Luke had a flashback to being bullied, both physically and verbally, for months after school by Darren Pritchard and his gang of cronies. Luke had been around ten years old and Pritchard fourteen. It had got so bad he finally broke and told Tom. A few days later, Connor had visited Burmantofts for the weekend and he, Tom and Luke went to a recreation ground—'the rec'—to play football.

Afterwards, Luke spotted Pritchard with several of his cohorts on the rec's lower level in the park at the far corner. After the situation had been explained to his thirteen-year-old cousin, Connor—insisting to Tom that he handle it due to being a similar age to

Pritchard— marched over and challenged the bigger, taller youth to a fight.

Soon Connor slid around the flailing Pritchard, hitting him with smacking jabs to the face and wind-sucking ones to the body. Even at ten years old, Luke knew Connor was prolonging the beating and taking pleasure in humiliating the bully. His elder cousin danced around his victim like Sugar Ray Leonard, winding up the right hand then smacking him with the left, standing in front of the windmilling boy with his hands behind his back making him miss like Roy Jones Jr.

Only when Pritchard raised his arms in defeat, did Connor use his right hand and left hook to floor him.

That was when Connor removed his belt and began to whip the cowering Pritchard without remorse across the face, the protective hands and then the back of his head.

None of Pritchard's friends intervened despite making feints to.

It had been the Ryder cousins' Uncle Michael, sent to pick them up, who cut through the crowd to snatch up Connor and end it. Luke remembered his cousin laughing at Pritchard's sobbing.

Luke answered Bill, "Let's hope he can restrain himself."

11

Mark felt more relaxed than he ever had before in Fred's office at the scrapyard. He nursed his cup of tea on top of his belly—one of the rare occasions Fred had ever made him one.

The family patriarch had been outlining his plans for the family, which was something Mark could never remember him discussing with him before. He thought back to all those times when Fred would keep Andrew behind after dismissing him. Now, he was being included in these conversations and it felt good.

His older brother began wrapping up the conversation with, "Well, our Nat will have the party they deserve, thanks to you. You did a good job. Sorry I've made ya meet me so late, but I've been rushed off my feet today."

"No, no. It's OK. I was busy with things too," lied Mark; he had been watching TV while eating crisps.

Fred stood up, patted him on the arm, and said, "Leave your cup. I'll wash it up."

Mark bounced out into the crisp, dark night. The scrapyard resembled a mass grave for cars, their rusted, eyeless chassis stacked on top of one another. Days earlier, he had bought an Audi Q5 sports utility vehicle with tinted back windows and barely fifteen thousand miles on it. He enjoyed the smell, the performance, and that he sat higher in it than most car drivers. He had looked around the showroom and wondered if he might ever own a new-car garage himself. He liked the shininess of regimented row upon row of brand-new models, and could see himself in a shirt and tie, badgering people into buying; he would be good at it.

He turned the corner, and got into his new toy. Inhaling the smell of the fresh valet, he fired up the engine and set off home.

As Radio 1 filled the car, he pulled out onto the quiet road and remembered he had a bag of Liquorice Allsorts in one of the carrier bags full of shopping he'd done a few hours earlier.

He reached back and began feeling for them before setting his hand on the plastic wrapper.

Stuffing a couple of his favoured, pink-dotted jelly spog sweets in his mouth, he felt a joy on how good life was at the moment. The professional job he had done on that old couple and their dog still filled him with pride. As the gelatine glided on his tongue, he remembered how the old bitch's face dropped when he had snapped the hind leg of the yapper and thrown it onto the sofa—though he had been aiming for the door.

He placed a hand on his belly as it rumbled, and hoped his gas would settle before he got home; he fancied a shag tonight.

The street lights petered out as he reached his house. He hadn't long moved into the posh area, and liked that the uptight neighbours hated his being there.

His nose wrinkled when he saw his work van, how cheap and dirty it looked in comparison to his new Audi.

He turned into his driveway and clicked the garage door remote, enjoying it peeling back under his power.

Driving in, he fumed on seeing that the metal storage cupboard at the far end, near the access door, had been pushed out a couple of feet and sat at an angle.

How fucking hard is it to push it back after she's fucking cleaned? I've got the shopping. Give her an inch and she takes a fucking mile.

A smile crept over his face, knowing he'd have to give her a slap before any sex could commence.

He switched the engine off, killing a girl band song and got out. He stomped his way to the cupboard.

Then froze.

The Balaclava stepped from behind it with a long-barrelled pistol levelled at him.

"Close the garage door."

When his brain failed to process the scene, the man stepped closer and stabbed at him with the sentence, "Close the fucking door. Now!"

Mark pressed the button in a panic and the roller door began to rumble down.

Crackling ice branched out through his frame as he began to be trapped with this man.

"Turn around and kneel."

"Please…please—"

"Shut the fuck up, you fat tub of shit. This is a suppressor. The next time you don't do exactly what I say, when I say it, you'll say goodbye to one of your kneecaps. If I wanted to kill you, you'd be dead. Now be a good boy and do as you're told."

Hope plumed inside him, as he had thought the man was going to kill him on the spot. He spun around and knelt.

"Drop your keys, wallet and phone. Lay down. Cross your wrists behind your back."

Mark complied, despite his nerves fraying as his belly pancaked out on the cold ground. The Balaclava scraped up the phone, wallet and keys, before a zipping sound bit into Mark's wrists.

"Lift your head and shut your mouth."

Mark's brain had unscrambled enough to recognise that though northern, the voice wasn't from Hull.

The silver adhesive tape strapped around his mouth like it was alive.

"Get up. If you make a sound from here on in, you'll die. Nod if you understand."

When he did so, the voice said, "Get up and walk slowly to the boot of your new car."

He heaved himself up, surprising himself at how much effort was needed to do so. He wandered over and peered into the abyss.

The Balaclava said, "I understand it's going to be a tight squeeze for a *Jacamo* shopper. But you're getting in there even if I have to break your fucking legs. So get to it."

Like a cross between a newly born foal and a hippo, Mark awkwardly struggled in. Finally, with his thighs against his belly, and chin pressing against a concertina of fat, he was in.

"Get comfortable. It'll be a while. If you're good, I reckon you'll be back here before midday tomorrow. If you're bad, the last thing you'll see will be my face."

Curtis quietly ate the shepherd's pie his mum, Joanne, had made. He sat across from his twin brother, Charlie, who sat to the left of his sister, Katie. Joanne sat at the head of the table. Back in the 'old days'—before his dad's death—his mum would be seated on Curtis's left. At the head of the table would be his dad, or left empty during his time in prison.

It annoyed Curtis that she sat there now. A dark blue cloth covered the table. A picture of where the sand meets the sea on a sun-soaked tropical beach hung above the fish tank behind Katie and Charlie. He was the last one to finish, and placed his cutlery on his plate.

Yesterday, he had driven to Lambert Transport Ltd to pick up a brick of cocaine he had hidden around the back of the main building months prior. Just before he rounded the corner he had overheard Luke and Bill Hopkins talking about him.

"Connor might handle it so it doesn't come back on the family. Like I said, the guy is a mong but needs a lesson," had said Luke.

"What do you think young Connor will do?" Bill had asked.

"Well, Tom's asked him not to go too far, so maybe he'll break legs or something. We'll see."

It was at that point a black cat had butted against his leg, and Curtis had kicked it without thinking before sliding away with his heart freezing in his chest.

"Are you OK, Curtis, love?" asked his mum, interrupting his thoughts. "You've barely said a word all night."

"Am fine."

"You know what your dad used to say: 'bring it to the table, and we'll discuss it as a family', so if—"

"I. AM. FINE," he exclaimed. "Dad isn't here any more, is he? I've come over for my tea, not an interrogation."

Katie tongue-lashed him with, "Who the fuck do you think you're talking to? Mum's made tea for us all and was only asking after you."

"And I told her twice, I am fine."

"Who's *her*? The cat's mother?"

"Fuck off, Katie."

His sister drew breath, but before she could cut into him, his mum said, "Let's all calm down and not ruin the evening."

After a moment's silence, she asked, "Want to help me in the kitchen, Katie?"

His mum collected his plate, and Katie picked up Charlie's, before hissing, "Punk," and following her into the kitchen.

Charlie looked at him. "What the fuck, Curtis?"

"Not you as well? Every fucker is on me."

"Eh?" said Charlie. "Like who?"

Curtis sighed. "Tom. He's ragging me about these guns in Leeds and the shooting. I am hitting a brick wall."

His twin nodded. "He's under a lot of stress himself. This gun thing, the new lap dancing club, all the usual aggravation, and on top of this, some cowboy builder from a gangster family in Hull ripped off one of Gran's friends."

Curtis's forehead scrunched. "What gangsters?"

"The Troys. I don't know what Tom wants to do about it yet—might not be worth the aggro. Then again, Connor is back—you know what he's like."

Connor took the balaclava off, and switched off his target's phone before sticking it inside one of the pockets of a work jacket hanging in the cupboard he'd hidden behind.

Next, he got into the driver's seat, donned a baseball cap, opened the garage door and fired up the engine.

He knew this was a dangerous phase of the operation. If Mark Troy's girlfriend popped her head out of a window to investigate why her boyfriend had come into the garage just to go back out again, then his plan could go awry.

He had observed the house for a few nights and discovered she turned in around ten. Still, a few nights' routine couldn't be relied on to be confident of a permanent pattern. However, he had seen the lights go off earlier before entering the garage, so held his nerve. If she was awake, the girl would have heard the vehicle as she had opened the bedroom window on the previous nights to let out the smell from the spliff she smoked just before turning in.

He flicked down the Audi's visor to afford him some degree of anonymity should she look out, but kept his eyes on the curtains as he edged the Q5 out.

Clicking the button, the door seemed to taunt him with how slow it was taking to unfurl down. Finally shut, he reversed out of the driveway.

His heart kicked on seeing the flicker of the curtain. As he sped away, he thought—*I hope that was the breeze coming in.*

Mark fought against the suffocation of his cramped position. With his weight pressing on them, his wrists were crying out under the bite of whatever secured them.

The Q5 sped up, forcing him against the back. He started to imagine the boot unlatching and being thrown out.

After a time, it got to the point where he longed for the journey to end, even though he did not know what would happen. He tried to distract himself from the pain by running through hopeful scenarios in his head.

It'll just be a shakedown. Whoever this is will call my brothers for a ransom. They'll pay and job's a good'un.

Soon after this thought, a thorn grew in his brain—*I am going to be known as the one who got himself captured. I'll be back at the bottom. They'll treat me like a kid again.*

He felt like crying with frustration.

The journey seemed to be taking forever. His body listed back as the vehicle slowed, but the bumps vibrated through him, making his teeth chatter.

Finally, the inertia slowed and then stopped. Fear washed over the relief.

The cold night air rushed in with the opening of the boot. The pistol came into view with the balaclava-framed blue eyes behind it.

"Come on, big boy. The sooner you move, the sooner you'll be in the warm."

The Hull native began to struggle his frame up, before flopping his legs out. He stood, stretching his back out, as he looked around.

A row of metal storage containers stood, lined up, ten metres in front of him. To his left lay the long, winding, rocky road they had driven up. The lights of a distant village shone a beacon in the black landscape.

To his right, around seventy metres away, was some kind of quarry.

"I understand I've been fat-shaming you, for which I apologise, but don't try and run, unless you can run faster than a bullet."

The Balaclava walked over to the second container on the left and opened it up. Inside, it had a chipboard floor. A black holdall nestled in the corner like a sleeping reptile.

His kidnapper ushered him forward and inside with his pistol. Mark began to shiver as he stepped over the threshold.

Once inside, the door creaked, closing to create pitch black all around him. A click stabbed light into his eyes, and he scrunched them up.

"Lay down on your front."

The Hull criminal attempted to turn around to protest, but a boot knifed into the back of his right knee. The palm strike between the shoulder blades threw him forward, and the chipboard rushed up to smack the right side of his face.

"Things will be easier if you just do as you're told, when you're told."

A zipping bite snatched his ankles together.

Then the figure stepped over him and opened the black bag.

He stood, but obscured whatever he had taken out by walking backwards. As the man disappeared behind him, Mark began to shift, only to find a boot pressing on his neck.

"You silly billy, Mark. If you ever had a chance to escape, it would have been in the first five seconds of capture. Not now, with your wrists and ankles tied in the middle of nowhere."

The logic of the words hit him hard. The voice continued, "I am going to do my James Bond villain bit, where I tell you exactly how clever my dastardly plan is. I like that word—dastardly."

Mark's stomach pancaked further out as the man sat on him, and continued, "I bought three boxes of these metal rods for punching letters into different types of material. Each contains thirty-six rods. I had to buy three of 'em because the three words I have sorted them into have a couple of the same letters. I have superglued the rods into the arrangement I want along with the end of a flathead screwdriver to make a dash—punctuation and that. Now, I will show you something, and if you start fidgeting when you see it, I'll use it on you. If you keep still, I won't. Do you understand?"

When he didn't respond, he felt a metallic edge clang into the back of his head.

"Mmpppphhhh," came his acknowledgement against the masking tape, along with an awkward nod.

He felt the pleasant sensation of stroking fingers on his neck, and the voice said softly, "I like this tattoo, Mark…two black birds…The Airlie Birds? Oh, the rugby team. Guessing you haven't played in a while; I bet when a waitress hands you a menu you just say 'Yes'."

A gun-like device appeared with a blue cylinder attached underneath with 'Butane/Propane' emblazoned on it. It took him a few seconds for his brain to compute it was a blowtorch. Remembering the man's words, he fought to keep still.

The blowtorch disappeared from sight. He jumped as the sound of fire-wind clicked on.

"I told you to relax. I am not going to use it on you."

The Balaclava switched his position so his knees were shunted up tight against Mark's armpits.

Sweat droplets crept out of the heavier man's follicles, like soldiers from trenches.

After a minute, the noise stopped and the blowtorch sat in front of his eyes.

A vice-like grip snatched his left ear as sixteen ends of burning metal seared into his right cheek.

The masking tape muffled his agonised roars. His left ear threatened to tear from his head as he thrashed. His bladder panicked into releasing itself.

Finally, the burning metal and pressure on his back were gone.

"There, there, all done," chirped the voice, like a nurse who had administered a vaccine.

Mark's breaths came out of his nose like seal snorts. He could smell cooked pork. Calming, he saw the Balaclava clutching his stomach, his body shaking.

He's laughing.

Eventually, the man stiffened. He said, "I am going to release your ankles and leave now. Count to one hundred slowly—that's ten, ten times—and then you can walk out. If you walk out before then, I'll shoot you."

He took out Mark's wallet and frisbee'd it at his head.

"Use your hard-earned money to get home. Walk back down the road until some kind soul lets you use their phone for a taxi. I'm sure you've insured your new Audi Q5—be against the law not to have."

The Balaclava squatted on his haunches, tore pain across Mark's mouth by removing the tape and added, "When your brothers ask you what I said, you're going to say, 'He just said you two would know what it was about'. That way they will think they are to blame, and won't turn it into a witch-hunt among all the people you've been in contact with. And they'll think of you as less of a pleb than they already do. Understand?"

Mark nodded.

"Good, let's practise."

"Wha…what?"

A rough hand snatched him by the hair and wrenched his neck taut. "I said, let's practise. Or are you deaf as well an insecure, bullying cunt?"

They practised a couple of times—like Andrew had made him do before the old couple—and the man let go of his hair. "Believe me, if politics hadn't got in the way, I'd have chopped off your fucking feet. Let this be a lesson to you—don't hurt or rip off the vulnerable, and we won't ever have to meet again."

12

Tom stood, leaning over the balcony of the lap dancing club undergoing refurbishment.

He watched Cara conversing with the architect, feeling a sense of pride at seeing all the workmen giving her sly glances.

Tom didn't blame them; her flawless mixed-race, caramel skin, chocolate eyes, shiny black hair and an uncommonly round ass drew looks wherever she went.

She finished up her conversation and made her way up to him, placing her hand on his shoulder.

"Happy?" he asked.

She nodded. "I think it's going to be great."

"Of course it will." He smiled.

"What's wrong?"

"What do you mean?"

"I can always tell."

He briefly raised his eyebrows. "Yeh. And you always know I won't tell you unless it's something that you can fix."

"Couples are meant to be able to talk to one another, Tom."

He frowned in exasperation. "This is what you signed up for. I told you that at the beginning, so you can't pout now, woman."

"At barely thirty years old you're waaaayyyy out of the generation of men to be referring to their girlfriend as 'woman', so it's Cara to you. Especially since I make my own money."

"OK…Cara…I told you at the beginning I would tell you what I can tell, but I can't tell you everything. It's not my fault you thought you could break me."

Connor's appearance behind her caused Tom to cut her retort off with, "Christ, are you ninja-trained or something?"

His cousin simply smiled. "How are you, Cara?"

"Am good, Señor Reed. How are you?"

Tom could see the beginnings of a smirk appear on his mouth; Cara was the only one who complied with his wish to be known as Connor Reed rather than Connor Ryder. It gladdened Tom they appeared to like one another; although they didn't have a playful ease together, as they had only met a handful of times.

"I am also good."

"Well, I will leave you to it."

"Yeh," said Connor, thumbing behind him. "Be a good WOMAN and get back to your embroidery."

Tom took an intake of breath, which he released on Cara's laughter. Connor gave a mock flinch as she walked past him.

Once she had disappeared, Tom said, "So, when I say it, I get told off for being sexist, but when you say it, it's funny."

"It's all in the delivery."

"You want a drink?"

"I'll make them," said Connor. "Coffee or tea?"

"Coffee."

Though faint, Tom detected a smell of petrol on him. Drinks made, they sat in a booth opposite one another.

"They're throwing up this place, aren't they," Connor observed.

"Had some rat problems. Cara doesn't know. Sorted now."

"What did you use? Poison? Traps? Cats?"

"Nah, Hughie came down with a few of his lads. Fuck me, there were loads of 'em—rats, I mean. Hughie's lads released these ferrets who went through the floor boards on a killing spree. When the rats jumped out to escape, the terriers caught 'em and ripped 'em to bits. Never seen anything like it—barely ten minutes and that's them gone. The lads collected 'em all and took off."

"All's well that ends well," said Connor.

"How was your trip away?"

Connor sipped his coffee. "I achieved everything I wanted to achieve, in the way we wanted to achieve it."

Tom knew this meant he had kept his identity hidden.

"Like you said, all's well that ends well."

"Seems that way."

"Will you be going anywhere, anytime soon?"

"I don't have plans to at the moment, but I suspect that will change."

"All right. You up to much while you're here?"

"Well, I've got some bits and bats to do. Got a date later in the week."

"Who?"

"A banker. Stephanie."

"How did you meet her?" asked Tom, curious. "A dating app?"

His cousin smirked. "You introduced us. Remember the black lady who showed me around the party you were hosting at the mansion? Do you still run those?"

Connor was referring to Tom's business venture, where he had bought a mansion not far from where they both now lived in Alwoodley. The elder cousin had used it for private parties for the affluent who wanted to indulge themselves with discretion. Tom would leave drugs in a room for those guests who wanted to partake. He had also separated the upper floors into bedrooms for sleeping and bedrooms for fucking in. It was in one of these bedrooms that Connor had 'met' Stephanie.

"I've had to put them on the back burner for now, with everything going on. I'll be honest, I underestimated the price of the upkeep of a house that size. With everything that's happening, I've been struggling to get a guest list together. As you know, they all need vetting."

"I see. Is there anything you want a hand with while I am here?"

Tom blew his cheeks out. "We've got a bit of— a lot of—an issue."

"All right."

"As you know, we've got a kinda protective umbrella up around us from the local law around here. Have had since your dad's day, and I did my best to maintain it even when Derek was fucking everything up."

Tom was referring to their uncle—since deceased—who proved to be an insecure, and egomaniacal leader.

The elder Ryder cousin continued with, "The local government and big businesses have plans for the city—I am talking millions and millions of investment, and they don't want it tarnished with negative press attention with fannies running around with guns."

"OK."

"This shooting has got everyone in a flap. They are going to steer the attention towards Bradford and hope it dies down. Thing is, one of our little scouts told Luke there've been bangs going off in Chapeltown and a rumoured one in Harehills. No one has died or even reported to the *ozzy*, and they have been reported as fireworks. But this lad said he's found the empty casings. Police don't know about this yet."

"Had any sniffs on who it might be?"

"Not yet."

"Who have you got on this?"

"Curtis," answered Tom, before looking at his favoured cousin. "He's meant to be our eyes and ears on the estates since we've moved Luke up. I wanted to give him a chance to climb up in the family's graces again with a win."

"The more I hear about Curtis, the more I reckon that if he fell in the shower, he'd try and grab the water to stop himself."

Tom's smile didn't reach his eyes as he replied, "He's had over a week now. At first, I didn't want to ring around the people he was meant to be talking to cos I didn't want him thinking I was undermining 'im. But I brought 'im in to make sure he knew the severity of the situation."

"And how was his manner?"

Tom shook his head. "I didn't like it. Has an attitude he can barely hide. So I made the calls to these local snouts and—"

Connor interrupted with, "And he hasn't contacted any of them."

Tom sighed. "Correct."

"Leave him on it. Give me a couple of days."

"Don't do anything to 'im, Connor."

"Please," replied his cousin, with his eyes briefly narrowing. "I know what family means."

Mark—back in Fred's scrapyard office—felt the branding on his face burn again. It was as if the eyes of his brothers were microscopes, narrowing the sunlight into scorching rays.

"It's too high to even grow the fat cunt's beard over it," Andrew spat venomously.

"I don't know if even a tattoo would cover it properly," answered Fred.

They were back to talking about him as if he wasn't present.

It was now one o'clock in the afternoon and he hadn't had much sleep. When his tormentor had left, Mark had dutifully counted to one hundred, then another to be sure. After flinchingly sticking his head out of the container, he saw his Audi Q5 ablaze in the darkness a hundred metres down the track. The former rugby player had begun to jog towards it, but his breath gave out before realising the tank might explode. He wandered back to the container to think, only to be awakened by the light of dawn.

He had made the arduous trek to the village, to find salvation in a milk delivery crew. Looks of horror appeared on their faces as their eyes focused on his right cheek. And he knew they could smell the dried piss on him.

They called him a taxi.

When he got back, he could not work out the words, as they were reversed in the mirror's reflection. He used his cue-ball-white girlfriend's phone to take a picture of the grotesquely molten brand. His heart had pounded on looking at it:

RIP-OFF
MERCHANTS

"He said he doesn't know who did this. Whoever it was, was wearing a balaclava. His burnt-out Audi had the number plates removed. Fuck knows how the police hadn't arrived to it. Lucky it's a Sunday and the quarry isn't open. This thick bastard decided to leave it there and go to bed."

Fred stared at him, his eyes ablaze. "You fucking what? What would you have done if the coppers turned up at your house? What would you have said? 'Sorry, I didn't notice it was gone, I was too busy branding my own face'!"

Mark began with, "I…err…just thoug—"

"Shut up!" shouted Fred, before turning to Andrew. "This gets 'round someone has pinched him out of 'is garage and done that to him, our partners in Newcastle and Liverpool will be pissing themselves. Can you find out who's done this? All he's been doing is turning over old and disabled people. It must be someone naughty that's trying to aggravate us through picking 'im as a soft target."

"Maybe one of them is related to someone?" Andrew suggested.

"Can't see some old biddie being related to someone like that. It's someone our end wanting to make a statement," said Fred, before addressing Mark. "Oi, fuckhead. What did he sound like?"

"N…not from here—"

"We fuckin' know that. No one from 'ere would dare."

"He sounded more like a *Wezzy*."

"White? Paki? What?"

"He was wearing gloves but I think he was white…yeh, definitely white."

"Did he give you a reason?"

Mark shook his head. "He said you two would know what it was abart."

Fred looked at Andrew. "Any ideas?"

The middle brother shook his head with a frown. "Nah. I'll put the feelers out. Have a solid contact out that way. I know just how to play him."

13

Curtis stood, facing his benefactor, between their two vehicles in a pub car park near Castleford. The pub was painted white and, through the black wooden window frames, he could see the patrons not having a care in the world, as his heart tumbled into his stomach.

He gripped the inside of his jacket pockets in despair, as Andrew Troy continued talking.

"So, you see, young Curtis, I'll be severing our little partnership. I can't have you being late and missing calls. It was you who came to me, remember, and I've given ya a fair chance."

"You're fuckin' joking me," exclaimed Curtis. "You've put some war criminal psycho on me, and now you're fuckin' me off?"

"If you hadn't been late again, he wouldn't have grabbed you for a 'partner', which you'll never be, you'll just be his dog now," spat the older man. "And if he finds out I'm supplying you directly over his head then…well, you've seen yourself."

"Why don't you shop him to coppers—he'll be an illegal."

"Because if he even suspects it's me, he'll kidnap my daughter, rape her before setting her on fire. Believe me I've done my research."

"He'll be locked up though."

Troy hissed, "But the fucking others won't be, will they."

In an effort to bring him back on side, Curtis said, "I shouldn't have been late and that. Things have been a little hectic, that's all. I've still got three of the Glocks to get rid of. Surely you want the money for those? Please, give me another chance. They won't ever find out am dealing on the side. If my own family don't know, then a foreigner who's been here for two minutes won't."

Troy looked at him, and then looked up, seemingly into the treetops where the birds were chirping mockingly.

"I'll tell you what I am going to do is give you a chance to get back in. Little jobs, like, and you'll be paid, and in time I might start trusting you more."

"You're going to lose money now you don't have me supplying the guns. Even if you try and get other people, my family will be all over it, believe me."

Andrew smirked. "Let's not pretend you were shifting massive money. Last thing I want is the Ryders—the real ones—getting on my case."

Curtis felt a stab in his stomach when he said 'the real ones'.

Andrew continued, "There is one thing you can do for me. Keep your ear to the ground. My brother, Mark, was kidnapped a couple of days back by a group that might 'ave come from your neck of the woods. He managed to fight them all and they ran off, but not before they've put this brand on his face. I badly want to know who was behind it."

Curtis felt hope sing in his stomach. "How much is this information worth?"

"A lot."

"Enough for me to get my gun-running round back?"

He saw the older gangster's mouth twitch.

"If I thought you knew who it is for sure, I'd have considered it. But I reckon you're bullshitting, and you'll give anyone up. So, I aren't taking the risk."

The words burst from Curtis's mouth as Andrew began to turn away. "What if I said that it wasn't a group like you said, but only one man?"

Curtis saw his lifeline freeze before turning to him. "Go on."

"Do we have a deal?"

"I said I'll consider it. Now, go on."

"It was my cousin, Connor. I am telling you. And I am telling you, the rest of my family had nothing to do with it. He's like a wild dog."

The look of concern appearing on Troy's face momentarily confused Curtis. Then he understood.

"He'll trust me. I am his cousin. I can get him to a time and place you want, and bang, it'll be easy."

"You want us to kill your cousin?"

Curtis's thought process stopped, then rebooted.

"No, you could permanently disable him so he's not a threat. I dunno, crush his legs, so he never walks properly again. People are only scared of him because of what he can do physically."

"It's not that simple. If they know it's us, then the Ryder family goes to war, and that's a very expensive row to have over my halfwit of a brother."

Curtis gave a triumphant smile. His pitch spewed forth with hardly a breath taken. "Our Tom might run the family, but Connor is the one who has formed all the international contacts and that. And he's the one people are most scared of. You could take those contacts when he's disabled. Share 'em out with the lads from Manchester, Liverpool or whoever.

No one will touch you, not even my family. If Connor is gone, I'll pump loads of drugs and guns in. Tom won't ever believe it's me—and even if he does, he won't do owt to a family member."

"Your Uncle Derek is missing, presumed dead. You saying Tom Ryder had nothing to do with that?"

"I am telling you that will have been Connor. Even our grandad used to say he's a law unto himself. The only reason Tom would have had to go along with it is Derek had Uncle Greg, Connor's dad, killed. My cousin Tom wouldn't harm, let alone kill, a family member."

"What about you? Look a bit suspect we put him in a wheelchair and do nothing to you?"

Curtis shrugged. "Give me a bit of a kicking. But you can say he was the one you were really after for kidnapping your brother and doing whatever to him for no reason."

"All right," said Andrew, nodding slowly, before opening the boot of his car. He took out a package and handed it to him. "You've redeemed yourself a little. I've been wondering where to stash this. It's a gift for my sister, but she isn't out for another three days, so you're going to hold it for her."

"What…wha…OK."

Andrew laughed. "Good fucking boy for not asking, but I'll tell ya anyway. It's a customised CZ 75B Shadow Semi-Automatic 9MM handgun. Instead of being black, it's silver, with a redwood pistol grip. She's always had taste like that."

Curtis thought for a moment. "Not being funny, but if you're edgy about being caught with it, why would you get it for your sister?"

Andrew sighed. "Because what my sister wants she gets. It's always been that way. Which is why you'll fucking die if anything happens to it. Got it?"

"Got it."

"Keep the money for those Glocks for yourself, and keep by your phone."

Tom arrived at his Aunt Joanne's house and found his cousin, Katie, there too. He hadn't visited them in a while, and they made a fuss of him.

Pictures of the twins, Katie and Michael, decorated the room. He smiled at the photograph of his deceased uncle with his arm around Mike Tyson and remembered what his boxing fanatic uncle had said when introducing him to it.

"Told you that fucker was nowhere near the six-foot or five-eleven they put him at. He's five-eight, five-nine at most. That's what people don't understand, Terrell Briggs—six-foot-four, Tony Tucker—six-five, and Tyson knocked fuck out of 'em. Couldn't hit him, you see, head moving all the time. Skill underrated. Knocked out Spinks with a body shot from the southpaw stance."

The right-hand side of the comfortable cream settee, which had its fair share of tea and snack stains, sucked Tom into it.

Katie sat on the other side and Joanne on the two-seater with her legs curled underneath.

When she had turned the volume on the television down, he asked, "How's things, Joanne?"

"Good. We're managing. Well, more than managing. Just hard, sometimes. I think it's affected Curtis the most out of us all."

Katie interjected with, "You can't keep letting him off, Mum. We're meant to be pulling together."

Tom braced himself. "What's gone on?"

Though he was looking at Joanne, it was Katie who answered. "He's got a constant attitude. You'd think he was Justin Bieber or something. Mum made a lovely shepherd's pie, had us all over, and he's snapping like a brat at her."

Joanne said, "Been around to his house to drop some tea off and see if he wants his washing doing but he hasn't been there."

Tom shifted on the sofa. Wishing to soften the mood, he said, "How's Charlie?"

Joanne replied, "Charlie's great, isn't he, nothing is too much hassle. I hope Curtis snaps out of it soon. He used to be such a happy-go-lucky lad."

"How's Connor, Tom?" asked Katie, her demeanour lightening up, as she always seemed to when talking about, or being in Connor's presence. "Settling into his new house?"

"Well, he's been away on one of his trips. But he's back now. Probably making the place feel like home, as we speak."

On the coffee table were strewn vintage naked girl cards. Two glasses of whisky faced one another—one nearly empty and the other barely touched, separated by a pair of blue-lensed aviator sunglasses.

Connor watched the full lips stretched around him, with the large brown eyes refusing to leave his face.

Her hair seemed almost art-like, with the tight braids on the sides giving way to a two-part Afro on top.

Her right palm on his chest pressed him back into the sofa, her nails gently running across his pectoral Superman tattoo. Her left hand cupped his balls with a wet finger pressing against his arsehole.

Top three…definitely…fuck, no, she's The Queen at this, he thought.

He felt a surge of pleasure and pushed her away. She sat on her haunches and exclaimed in her London accent, "What's the matter?"

"Nothing. I want to fuck you, not cum in your mouth."

He seized her by the arms, but as he walked her to the sofa, she stopped him and raised her eyebrows.

"Take me upstairs, it's not like we met on Tinder."

He frowned, despite his arousal. "We met at a drug-fuelled orgy, Steph. Maybe we shouldn't judge people on Tinder."

"Erm, we met at a high-class social event that cost a lot of money to attend, so I thi—"

"OK. OK. OK, let's go upstairs, am losing my hard-on arguing."

Later, lying in bed together, and when his heart rate and breathing had returned to normal, he looked at her.

Her dark skin seemed almost light against her near-black nipples. She turned, stroked his Superman tattoo again and asked, "When did you get this done?"

"It's a birthmark. Here it is an 'S' but back on my home planet, it stands for hope." She guffawed and he said, "Hey? When I asked you before we began necking off if you were on birth control, why did you ssshhhh me?"

She made eye contact and said, "I just thought it was time."

115

As his mouth fell open, she laughed, pointing at him. "Your face." When he smiled, she added, "Don't worry. I wouldn't let a white guy get me pregnant."

Unable to decipher whether she was joking or not, he commented, "Not very liberal, is it?"

"I never said I was a liberal. Why would I want a child that doesn't look like either of us?"

Her words surprised him. "No child looks fully like either of their parents. And some might describe it as the best of both worlds."

"Pfffttt, some, but not me. I am proud of my race and want it to continue. What's wrong with that?"

"Aren't we all the human race?"

"Aren't tigers and lions all big cats? They can breed into those crossbreeds, but that doesn't mean they should."

"They are called tigons if the tiger is the father, ligers if the opposite is true," stated Connor. "And I'll be letting the most statesman-like US president of recent years know of your thoughts."

She burst out with, "I do love Obama."

"Fucking hypocrite."

The ringing of his phone interrupted her retort. It was an unknown number.

"That might be him now," he said, before answering. "Yes?"

"Connor, it's Curtis. Am outside."

"Why didn't you knock on the door?"

"Am in the car. It's started to rain, and I didn't know if you were in. I'll come to the door now."

The call ended and he turned to Stephanie. "There is someone at the door. I might have to go out for a bit. Feel free to make yourself at home and stay the night. Or you can leave when you want; the door is self-locking."

He began to don his pants, jeans and dark blue T-shirt.

"Shame. I was looking forward to a full night of it."

"Can't be helped. Please do not steal."

"Why would I steal?"

"You know…because you're…a banker," he said, with a wink, and left before she could retort.

Making his way downstairs, he tapped on his phone screen to reveal security camera views around the house.

He grabbed his jacket from the closet. It felt heavy on one side with the item he had stolen the previous night.

He opened the door to reveal Curtis with the rain spotting his black jacket.

"What is it, mate? I am entertaining."

"I've fucked up. Fucked up bad. I need your help."

"Go on."

"Can I come in? Am getting wet."

"Are you deaf? I said I am entertaining, and this doesn't sound like a conversation we want overheard. Let's go into the garage."

They went through the side door. With his car in Tom's garage, his '95 Speed Triple stood as a centrepiece within the garage. His biking jacket hung near the door, with the helmet slotted into an open box-section next to it.

Curtis, beginning to fidget, took a few deep breaths, and confessed, "I've gone outside the family to do bits and pieces on the side."

He looked at Connor like a pet Labrador would at a scolding owner. When Connor didn't speak, he continued, "Andrew Troy over in Hull offered me work and I took it."

"What type of work?"

"Guns."

He cowered, only relaxing when Connor said, "Continue. If I want you to stop, I'll tell you."

"I know it's wrong and I want to stop. He wants to meet me tonight, so I am going to tell him, but I am…scared he's not going to let me go?"

"So, why have you come out to me instead of Tom?"

Curtis looked sheepish. "Because, I don't want him finding out what I've been doing."

"I see."

"And you're one of the only people they are scared of."

Connor looked at him. "When and where is the meet?"

"It's near the power plant in Drax. About thirty miles away. It's in just less than an hour. I can't afford him sending people around to my mum's if I'm a no-show."

Thunder sounded in the distance. Connor said, "Ever notice thunder sounds a bit like taking the wheelie bins out around the front in a morning?"

His younger cousin's forehead scrunched. "Wha…yeah, suppose."

Connor smiled, reached into his jacket and took out the custom silver CZ75B Shadow with a redwood grip.

Curtis's wide-eyed face drained of blood as he approached him. Connor clasped the back of his neck tightly, and placed the gun underneath his chin. "Daniel Day-Lewis would have been proud of that little performance, Curtis."

"Wha…what you talking about?"

"You have the awareness of a pissed-up sixteen-year-old girl on Es. You didn't even notice this—the thing Andrew Troy had specifically told you to keep hold of—has been missing from the boot of your car for nearly twenty-four hours, let alone the parabolic microphone I placed under your wheel arch days ago. You didn't even notice me in the car park when you were having your conversation with him. I especially liked the 'just crush his legs' bit."

"Please. Please. Please—"

Connor shouted saliva onto Curtis's face, "SHUT UP! Can't you even have a scrap of dignity?"

When Curtis quietened and stood a little straighter, Connor continued, "This CZ75 is a gift from God. That Kentucky Fried fuck fell for the BB gun with a silencer, but his brothers are a little more discerning. As you know, the Ryder family doesn't keep real guns at their residences in case of the law visiting. You must have forgotten."

"I just—"

"And you let some mini-me Milošević into our city whose first act was to shoot up a car of Asians, something that's causing untold drama," said Connor, pressing the barrel harder into his jaw. "The thing is, our Tom loves you like he does all the family. That's why he gave you the task of finding out who was bringing in the shooters. It wouldn't have occurred to him it was you—not until you made it blatantly obvious."

"I am sorry. It was just with…when I got shot…and how Luke and Charlie are your favourites. And—"

"We haven't got time for a therapy session. Just tell me the exact location and what the layout of it is."

Curtis let out an open-mouthed, stuttering sigh. "It's a disused factory where they fixed train chassis. I don't know how many guys he has with him." He gave Connor the exact address and postcode.

"Are these Serbs going to be there?"

"No. That Andrew doesn't want to be anywhere near them if he doesn't have to be."

Connor asked, "Will these Troys be armed?"

"I don't think so. I told them you wouldn't be. I reckon it'll just be a lot of heavies."

"Stay where you are. If you move, I'll break your neck and bury you up on Saddleworth Moor."

He took out his phone, dialled, and said to the voice answering, "It's a disused train repair factory in Drax. Can't be sure of the numbers or whether they'll be armed. I'll send you the postcode now and meet you there."

When he hung up, Curtis asked through his jitters, "Wh…who was that?"

Connor looked at him with pity. "Who do you think?"

14

Mark stood in the clinking dark of the factory. He felt a sliver of nerves in his stomach, awaiting the arrival of the man who had kidnapped and branded him.

He admonished himself. *Stop being a puff. He's the one who's getting it now.*

Andrew stood a step in front, in the clearing, facing the roller and side doors.

Hidden behind the derelict corner office block to his left was Fred, three of his enforcers, and a massive Cane Corso Manolo he had bred and trained in Poland.

The dog—just shy of nine stone—looked like a dirty jacket of grey fur had been forced over a frame of pure canine muscle. Mark had seen the dog reach his eldest brother's height when standing on its two legs with its front paws on his shoulders.

Its tail began wagging furiously and its head tilted up at Fred, who heeled it with a jerk of its chain lead. The combination of the muzzle and its training kept it still and quiet.

The sound of tyres crunching over the gravel outside filtered through the rainfall and roller door.

Andrew whispered, "They're here."

"We know," said Fred. "Spike here has already told us."

A few moments of damp quiet descended before the spherical side door knob rotated.

In stepped the man he knew to be Connor Reed. A thin, green leather jacket, black T-shirt and dark jeans encased his physique—he reminded Mark of the dog that was about to savage him.

The younger Curtis appeared next, closing the door behind him. No one had told him his cousin, Connor, would die tonight.

Andrew's voice cut through the building. "I wasn't expecting company, Curtis."

It was Connor who replied. "Yes you was."

The answer confused Mark, as Fred, Spike and the three lads came out of the shadows.

Fred's voice boomed, "The famous Connor Reed. I haven't met ya before. Mark 'ere 'as, but not me. And neither 'as Spike 'ere."

As Fred leant down to remove the beast's muzzle, Reed descended into a quarter-squat, whistled, slapped his knee and called out, "Come here, boy."

Fred pointed at the Leeds man, released the chain with a shout of, "Attack!"

With saliva-spraying and blood-curdling barks, the brute leapt at his prey. Reed's hand moved so quick Mark's brain could not compute it. The dog skidded with a mew, and shook its head violently before toppling to the ground in convulsions.

Mark's jaw hinges slackened as his eyes passed from the dog to Reed. He held a silver pistol levelled at Fred in his right hand. He let fall the Taser from his left.

"If any of you even fucking twitch, I'll start shooting. Believe me, against you set of fucking *doylems*, it'll look like a John Wick scene," he said, before giving the order of, "Curtis, let the others in."

The building began to blur for Mark, and he fought to keep his legs underneath him. He caught the look on his older brother's face, a look he had never seen on his family's leader before—fear.

Several men of all shapes and sizes entered and surrounded them. One removed the prongs from the dog and began taping its legs and jaws together.

Mark involuntarily sank to a sitting position on the floor.

The handsome one with bright blond hair sneered, "Fat cunt's legs deserve a medal for holding him up this long, to be fair."

Connor slid his gun back inside his jacket and addressed Fred. "Unless your dog has a heart condition of some kind, it should be fine. Can only get those bad boy Tasers from Ukraine."

Mark could hear the nerves in his eldest brother's reply. "What's going to happen now?"

"That sack of shit sat there, irrespective of the fact he likes to hurt defenceless people and animals, thought it would be a good idea to come into our city and rip off old ladies. Worse though, is Andrew 'The Walking Lamp Post' thought he could distribute guns in our city despite being told no."

Andrew interjected, "Curtis said it was OK."

In a movement too quick for Mark's eye to catch, Reed levelled the pistol at Andrew, who flinched.

"Tell another lie, I dare ya. I heard you with my own ears," Connor snapped. "Say sorry for lying."

"Am…am sorry for lying."

"I accept your apology. Depending on how the rest of this meeting goes, I'll find a way to get this gun back to you, Andrew, before your sister comes out. From the sounds of it, you're more scared of her than you are—were—of us."

Connor continued to address Fred. "Luckily, I don't make the decisions for the family, because if I did, you'd all die right now."

A man, a touch shorter, a bit broader than Connor, with darker hair, stepped forward.

He said to Fred, "You know who I am?"

Fred nodded. "Thomas Ryder."

"Your brothers have been fucking headaches. So reparations will need to be made," stated the Ryder clan leader. "But first, we have to deal with our common enemy."

"What common enemy is that?"

"Maybe your brother Andrew can tell ya—tell all of us."

The focus of the room shifted to the middle Troy brother.

Mark heard his brother enunciating his words, like he used to in the face of their father's wrath.

"I made some of the immigrants associates for low-level stuff like muling, or giving someone a smack, or if I wanted someone leant on. They were handy to keep distance. I haven't got the time to tell you how it got worse and worse. But this Serbian is here, and he's looking to take over."

Connor said, "Why haven't we got time?"

Mark could see his brother's back straighten. "Because he's on his way—I reckon you have two minutes. If you leave now I'll tell them you were a no-show, because believe me you don't want to be here when they arrive. And yes, they will be armed."

The sound of approaching cars in the distance filtered through the windows.

"That'll be them now."

Mark saw a smirk appear on his brander's face. "Please don't threaten me with a good time."

Despite his forced display of confidence, Connor felt his insides ice. Although he had thoroughly checked the CZ75's firing mechanism functioned and had cleaned the working parts, he had not fired it; therefore he did not know the differential between its point of aim and point of impact.

Only he was armed and there was only one exit.

With the immediate danger overcoming any hierarchal protocol, Connor commanded, "We haven't got time to escape. Tom, make sure none of these go for their phones."

"You can't go out there on your own. There could be loads of them."

"There's only one gun here. All anyone will be out there is targets. Besides, it's them who are getting ambushed."

Connor turned his back and headed to the door, as Tom commanded the lads take a grip of the Troys and their cronies.

The cold night air breezed the sound of the vehicles into his ears.

He bolted into the hiding arms of the treeline just as a black van and a dark blue saloon prowled around the corner.

Connor crouched and his focus burnt through the dark thoughts of failure's consequences. After swapping the pistol to his left, his right hand scooped up a fallen branch.

Five men alighted from the vehicles like the soldiers they were—spaced out and watchful. He immediately recognised who the leader was.

Dušan Dragojević got out of the van like a medieval king stepping down from a horse.

The black operations agent held his nerve as the former Serbian paramilitary soldier seemed to look right at him, before his gaze scanned the rest of the woods.

The former Royal Marine's heart pounded as one of the men approached the door before Dragojević had averted his gaze.

At the last moment, their leader looked away and Connor threw the branch high and hard.

Their heads whipped around as it smacked against the van's windscreen.

He fired three shots in a rapid sequence.

The first merely skimmed the ear of the furthest left target, but the readjusted second shot caught him in the face. The next tore through the throat of the next.

At this distance with his targets spread, Connor could not prevent Dragojević and his men whipping behind the cover of the vehicles.

He slid back and quickly ran twenty metres to his left, knowing his muzzle flash might have been seen. The sound of tree bark being hammered into splinters shocked him. He didn't hear the report of gunfire and realised his enemies must be armed with suppressed assault rifles.

Peering through the dark of the trees, and hearing the strange Serbian commands he saw they were attempting to hem him in with a tri-pincher.

Connor had observed coming into the area—around the size of half a football pitch—that industrial fencing with pointed tops enclosed it.

He stalked backwards, considering his options. Though there might be a chance of a gap in the fence, he could not bank on it, and the fencing was too tall to scale.

Come on, Connor—he thought—*don't let some fucking baddie kill you in Drax.*

Dragojević felt a smile play on his face as he crept between the dark trees. A certain disappointment tempered the familiar excitement of the hunt—he couldn't afford to attempt to take this man alive. The way he had gunned down Tomislav and Zoltan showed a great skill of shooting.

Still, the man was trapped now, and Dragojević hoped whoever shot the man first, merely injured him—after he had finished with the man, he'd have photographs taken as a warning to these soft British criminals.

As the rainfall whipped into him, the war veteran kept his eyes wide and scanning with the suppressor of his Uzi following his hawk-like gaze. Azem and Borisav—both to his left with Borisav furthest—maintained a line of sight, and it was a testament to their skills that they were systematically covering the ground rather than rushing.

Dragojević could now make out the fence line, and his anticipation rose as he realised his prey must be behind one of the trees.

He picked out the ones large enough to hide a man—there were two, and turned to gesture to Borisav and Azem.

Except Borisav had disappeared behind a tree. Dragojević halted Azem to wait for Borisav to reappear.

In the moment it took for his instinct to spin him around, an invisible mallet smashed through his knee, pitching him forward and prising the Uzi from his grip.

He fought the shock. His peripheral vision caught Azem's torso's bloody unzipping.

His left foot found purchase in the cold soil and pushed. Heaving his body forward like a beached seal, his clawing right hand landed on the Uzi.

In the same instant, bone shards exploded from the flesh pulp of his fingers.

His survival instinct rode over his horror to reach with his left.

The boot whipped the Uzi away from his grasp.

Dragojević's gaze rose to meet the blue eyes of the dark-blond, young man stood over him.

"There are a lot of people who would like you to be delivered to them, Dušan," said the man, with a smile. "But I don't think any of them will give you the send-off that I am going to."

15

Tom sat with Luke in the booth of the now fully refurbished lap dancing club, 'The Helena'.

In three days' time, it would have its opening evening.

"Looks awesome in here, Tom," said Luke, looking down through the glass at the alluring black stage, beige leather seating and 1940s style bar bathed in low amber light.

Tonight would be a rehearsal for their big opening.

"We'll get this out of the way so we can enjoy tonight," said the elder Ryder. "Remember, we'll both take turns speaking. This is how I want it from now on, so people see you as an authority in the family. Understand?"

"Yeh."

"Here they are now."

Oshain 'Bambi' Riley, a tall, handsome, mixed-race amateur MMA fighter and the head of their door security, ushered in Fred and Andrew Troy through the backdoor entrance of the club. He pointed to Tom and Luke, and the Troy brothers made their way up to them.

Tom didn't need to study their postures to know they were nervous. The fact they had answered his summons and were on time, indicated their newfound obedience.

Still, Tom and Luke stood to greet them. They shook hands, and the Troys took their seat across from the Ryders when Tom gestured for them to do so.

He didn't offer them a drink.

"We didn't get to finish our conversation back in Drax," said Tom. "What with having to get rid of the bodies of the men you brought over."

Andrew met his eye but Tom could see it was a struggle for him.

Fred turned his palms up. "We are here to make amends."

Luke said, "You own FTM Lettings Agency in HU1, and don't tell us otherwise. You're going to cut us in as silent partners for a pound. In exchange, I am going to take three points off all the properties' rental incomes, leaving you with the other seven."

The silence hung like a bat.

"For how long?" asked Fred.

"Forever. And it's on all current and future properties."

"That firm looks after hundreds of properties. That's fucking extortion."

"Up to you," came Tom's cold reply.

"A point and a half," asked Fred, with pleading eyes.

Tom looked at Luke, as rehearsed, who answered, "Two. And you're going to take on Curtis as a lettings agent."

Andrew stated, "To spy on us."

"Not entirely, Andrew," said Tom. "Curtis didn't betray you, he betrayed us. And we don't want him anywhere near our businesses. He can visit any family member who wants him to, but he isn't living in Leeds again. You agree to these terms, then it'll save a war between our families. And who knows, maybe we can do business in the future."

Fred and Andrew looked at one another briefly, before the eldest Troy said, "OK. Deal."

They stood and as the Ryders and Troys shook hands, Fred asked, "I take it we won't be seeing our Serbian friend anytime soon."

Tom replied, "That's safe to say."

Andrew asked, "What about your cousin Connor. Should we be expecting a visit?"

The shake in the voice made his words sound louder than they were.

Luke answered sharply, "If we're saying it's the end of it, then it's the end of it. Luckily for you, he's a very sweet man—until he's not."

Connor sat on the steps of the mansion in Alwoodley, taking in the scene of the huge lawn. He enjoyed the meditative effect of the blue lit cascading fountain made of oil jars forming its centrepiece.

The wheels of the silver Mercedes rolled over the gravel of the long driveway before stopping.

Three men got out: Arben Tinaj, the shadowy leader of the revamped Hellbanianz organised crime group, and presumably two foot soldiers.

The dark-haired, grey-eyed British-Albanian—around Connor's age, height and build—wore a tan suede coat over a grey woollen jumper, and smart jeans. A complete contrast, Connor thought, to his 'chavy', aggressive predecessor.

Connor stood and said, "How were your travels?"

"Straight up the M1, no messing," replied Arben. "Except I don't want to be up north any longer than I have to be."

The Yorkshireman smiled. "Follow me."

He led them around the mansion on the white stone path.

They reached the empty stables. Connor said, "The smell is going to hit you when I open this."

He slid back the bolt of the end storage compartment. The stench of chemicals, faeces, urine and sweat billowed out.

Dušan Dragojević hung by his wrists by a wrought iron chain straining against the eye-loop bolt to the ceiling. The thick black rope, wound around iron bars in front and behind the knees, riveted the legs straight.

He began to resemble a fish struggling on a hook as the light attacked his eyes, the tubing of the cannula attached to his arm flapping around. The insulated tape wrapped around his face like a silver snake.

His grime-matted clothes hung from his emaciated body. He had lost his feet, ankles, and legs from the mid-shin to the sizeable cylindrical vat of sulfuric acid beneath him.

A chuckle rode up Connor's diaphragm and escaped upon observing the horror and pain in the Serbian's eyes.

"Fack me," exclaimed Arben. "What have you done to 'im?"

"Just been lowering him in a few inches a day. He normally passes out. The funniest part is watching him come around again—it's like it takes him a second to realise where he is."

There were a few moments of silence before Arben spoke. "Why is he so skinny?"

"You wanted him nourished too? Been drip-feeding him enough liquids to survive."

"How long have you had him?"

Connor shrugged. "Ten days."

"Ten facking days? You could have just handed him off to us. You doin' it for the cred?"

"The cred? You're taking the recognition for this, remember. I just wanted to have fun with him. The only reason I am giving him up now is we are due to have guests in this place soon."

When Connor noticed Arben looking at him with wide eyes, he exclaimed, "What? You feel sorry for this evil cunt? Do you know what he's done to women and children? Mostly to women and children of your heritage."

"All right, I get it," said the London gangster. "What now?"

"It's up to you. We can drop him in, and the acid will help get rid of him. You can film it for your boss in the old country. Or we can cut off his head, you can send that. Or whatever you want."

The chirps of birds filled the quiet, before Arben spoke.

"It's just as well you're passing this off to us. It's like you said, parasites like this don't give a fuck about catching hold of a man's wife, girlfriend and kids, and torturing 'em."

"Luckily I don't have a wife, girlfriend or kids," answered Connor, holding back the cliché of 'not that I know of'.

"Anyway, I suppose I'll say thank you for this."

"No need to thank me. As I said, it was a pleasure."

16

Paulette kept the pride off her face as Rene blatantly admired Connor on opening her door to them.

Paulette stepped past her to hear her ask, "Are you not popping in for a cuppa, my love? I've just boiled the kettle."

"I haven't got much time, Rene. I'll be rushing to drink—"

Paulette interrupted him. "Then just blow on it a lot."

She saw his face crease as he said, "All right, Gestapo of beverage consumption, I'll have a black coffee, please, Rene. I'll come with you to see the new kitchen."

They made their way to the kitchen and Rene said, "Looks lovely, doesn't it? So pleased."

"They've done well with this," said Connor.

Rene busied herself with the drink-making. "I just hope they don't try it with anyone else. I was lucky to have a friend like Paulette."

Connor nodded. "It's not as if they go around with a brand on their face warning people who they are."

"I know. More is the pity."

She handed them their cups. "Let's go into the living room."

Rene led the way, with Connor bringing up the rear.

When the door opened, Paulette heard him take a snap of breath. She turned to find him stood stock still, looking at the graduation picture of Rene's granddaughter.

"Yes, she's a beauty. Stop prat-arsing around and come in."

He followed her in and sat on the sofa next to her. Rene sat on her chair beneath the pictures.

Paulette frowned—she hadn't seen him this…distracted before.

Rene looked up at the pictures of the stunning redhead and said to him, "That's my granddaughter Grace. That one is when she qualified as a paediatric surgeon. And that one is with her son, Jackson."

"Handsome devil, isn't he? Has my name too—Grace has given up her adoptive parents' name of Templeton, long story so it is, and taken our name of Lewis."

Connor slowly nodded. "How old is he?"

"He's only a few months."

"When's his birthday?"

Paulette asked, "Why do you want to know his birthday? Going to get him a card?"

He gave her a tight smile, and then asked, "If you don't mind me asking, is his dad on the scene?"

Rene shook her head. "I asked her once, and she wouldn't answer, so I never asked her again. She'll be around in five minutes, maybe you'll get more luck."

Paulette noticed Connor shift in his seat, before pulling out his phone.

"Rene. Gran. I've got to go. It isn't just because of this poorly made coffee." He smiled at Rene, who laughed. He set his cup down, and in a flash had given them both a kiss on the cheek before they had managed to stand up.

When he had left, Rene said, "Must be an emergency."

"Yes," murmured Paulette, looking at the picture of Grace and Jackson. "Must be."

"You must be proud of them all, Paulette."

"Of course I am." She nodded. "But what grandmother isn't."

There was a knock at the door, and before it opened a female voice lilted with a north-east accent sang out, "It's only me, Gran."

Paulette looked up to see the attractive redhead with a strikingly curvaceous figure appear. She gripped a white, baby-carrying basket.

Rene squealed, "Let's have a look at him then, Grace."

She reached into the basket and picked up the bright-eyed baby to whisper quiet adorations to him.

Grace crossed to the now standing Paulette, "You must be Paulette. Thank you for looking after my gran."

"That's what friends are for, love," said Paulette, her eyes fixed on Jackson.

"Would you like to hold him?" asked Grace.

Rene said, "I don't think that's Paulette's thing, Grace."

"Don't be hogging him, Gran, you've got all evening. Unless you don't want to?"

Paulette surprised herself by replying, "No. I'd like to."

Rene looked startled but gently handed him over.

As he stared up at her, she felt a confusing sense of warm familiarity.

AUTHOR'S REQUEST

Please leave a review of An Outlaw's Reprieve

As a self-published author, Amazon reviews are vital for me getting my work out as many readers as possible.

By reviewing it means I can continue to write these books for you.

Thank you so much

Quentin Black

An Outlaw's Reprieve

GLOSSARY

ABA— The governing body of amateur boxing clubs in England was known as the Amateur Boxing Association of England (ABA for short) until 2013. Now known as England Boxing.

ADCC— An acronym for 'Abu Dhabi Combat Club', a globally renowned grappling tournament.

Becket's Approval— After the Archbishop of Canterbury, Thomas Becket, had stoked the ire of Henry the Young King, the Monarch is said to have uttered the words, *"Will no one rid me of this turbulent priest?"*. His knights interpreted this as a wish for the priest to be killed.

Therefore a 'Becket's Approval' is an inference an assassination is desired without strictly saying so.

B-roads— distributor roads, which have lower traffic densities than the main roads.

Brock— Northern England slang for broke or broken.

Cob on— Northern England slang for being in a bad mood.

Comfer— Hull slang to refer to people from West Yorkshire who come to Hull for the weekend.

Doylem— Northern England slang for idiot.

Gobbed off— English slang for speaking out of turn.

Gorga— Romany gypsy slang for 'non-traveller'.

HMET— Homicide and Major Enquiry Team. An elite crimes unit that conducts investigations pertinent to West Yorkshire.

Jacamo— An online shopping company catering for large men.

Job's a good'un— Northern England slang expressing satisfaction a task has been or will be carried out successfully.

John Prescott— a British politician who once punched a protestor in retaliation for throwing an egg at his head.

Julie Andrews— With Milk but no sugar, as in 'White Nun'.

Lugholes— British slang for ears.

Mafting— Hull slang for hot.

Mithering— British slang for making an unnecessary fuss.

Mouse— Hull slang for going into a bad mood.

NCA— National Crime Agency; the UK's very rough equivalent of the US FBI.

On tag— Electronic monitoring (known as 'tagging') is used in England and Wales to monitor curfews and conditions of a court or prison order. If you're given a tag, it will usually be attached to your ankle.

Ozzy— Slang for hospital, originally deriving from Liverpool.

Pop my clogs— Northern England slang for die.

Prop forward— player who plays in a forward position on a rugby team. Forwards are generally bigger than the backs.

Pulling guard— to voluntarily assume the sitting position at the start of a grappling contest.

Rogue Traders— A British undercover consumer affairs television programme that targeted unscrupulous tradesmen who ripped off members of the public.

Ten-foot— Alley or passageway at the back or side of a building, usually 10 feet wide.

The Chase— a popular British television quiz show, 1995.

Twazzock— Hull slang for an idiot.

Weans— West Scottish slang for children. On the east coast of Scotland, the word bairn is more commonly used.

Wezzy— Hull slang for anyone from West Yorkshire.

Available on Amazon

The following is the second chapter of Quentin Black's

follow-up novel— *The Puppet Master*

Nineteen months ago

The two men stood side by side looking through the glass screen at the Danish surgical crew clad in either light aqua green or blue scrubs, masks and head coverings resembling shower caps. The medical team crowded the anaesthetised patient, obscuring him from view despite the bright overhead lights.

The Dane stood on the left—middle-aged, tall, light brown hair swept to one side of a face, though jowly when relaxed, was not fat. He inquired in English, "I realise I risk your anger asking, but I am a curious man, and your presence here would suggest that the patient is very valuable."

The Russian—similarly aged, a little taller, wavy brown hair and wearing a well-fitting suit with a touch of flamboyance, answered in the same tongue, "He has been a great servant to me—to my country. Whether he continues to be will be the result of your team's professionalism."

The Danish neuroscientist stiffened, "Their talent and professionalism are unmatched."

Despite the Russian's reputation, the jab at his team's—and therefore his—competence spurred him to answer. They were at the cutting edge of a bio-engineering technology called neuroprosthetics, helping to replace or assist damaged neurons, enhancing their function with external electrical circuitry. And their reputation for excellence had led to a substantial grant for the implementation of BCI—Brain-Computer Interface.

The Russian gave a subtle nod. "Calm yourself, old friend. The statement was not a threat. Tell me again of the…enhancement he will benefit from if this is a success."

The Dane partially relaxed. "If successful, the neural chip will be activated by the host's adrenal system. It will stimulate his vagus nerve and optimise his entire nervous system. The real innovation is that we've found a way of sending signals painlessly through the skin that selectively activate the optimal fibres while leaving the sub-optimal ones unchanged."

"You say it will work off his adrenal system. Will the neural chip be activated during a spoken argument?"

The Dane shrugged. "We have set the parameters high, so it can only be induced once a certain threshold of adrenaline is released—a combat situation, for example. Although, if it is triggered during an argument, the only thing likely to happen is that his verbal fluency, reasoning and decision-making will be enhanced. He will not be snapping the necks of parking attendants. It only acts to enhance his reflexes, sight, decision-making, physical and mental efficiency."

"All the things adrenaline heightens anyway."

"Yes, but not to this degree. And adrenaline only enhances the gross motor skills involving the legs, arms and trunk. It retards the fine motor skills of the hand and wrist."

"Why wouldn't someone want to be in this state as often as possible?"

"Because it'll cause a rapid drain on his body's nutrients, leaving him fatigued in the extreme."

The Russian turned to him sharply. "Leaving him vulnerable. How long would it take him to recover?"

"We have created vials of a formula—they trigger an initial release of CO_2 into his system. This tricks the haemoglobin molecules to dump oxygen for use by the muscles and brain, so they can transport the false CO_2 back to the lungs. There's also a concoction of protein nutrients, and iron. If he were to go into near-total depletion, post-injection revival to a 'normal' state should take a minute to ninety seconds. Full restoration to enable the enhancement should be no more than seven minutes."

The Dane mentally grimaced when the Russian asked, "You said 'near-total depletion'—

which suggests that if he is in this state too long he could die."

Inserting as much confidence in his voice as he dared, the Dane replied, "That is an improbable scenario."

"But possible."

"If he couldn't find the respite to inject himself, maybe. However, he will be like Superman for a short time, and so able to extract himself from the wrath of the Gods."

The Head of SVR RF (Foreign Intelligence Service of the Russian Federation) remained quiet for a moment. "There was once a time he could do so without enhancement. He is a little older now. Had a long career with many injuries. All men are human, but he is our best asset."

"Maybe with this he will be the first immortal," answered the neuroscientist. "Should he survive the surgery. As you are aware, no human subject has undergone this procedure."

ABOUT THE AUTHOR

+ Follow

Follow me on Amazon to be informed of new releases and my latest updates.

Quentin Black is a former Royal Marine corporal with a decade of service in the Corps. This includes an operational tour of Afghanistan and an advisory mission in Iraq.

AUTHOR'S NOTE

Join my exclusive readers clubs for information on new books, deals, and free content in addition my sporadic reviews on certain books, films and TV series I might have enjoyed.

Plus, you'll be immediately sent a **FREE** copy of the novella *An Outlaw's Reprieve*.

Remember, before you groan 'Why do I always have to give my e-mail with these things?!', you can always unsubscribe, and you'll still have a free book. So, just click below on the following link.

Free Book

Any written reviews would be greatly appreciated. If you have spotted a mistake, I would like you to let me know so I can improve reader experience. Either way, contact me on my e-mail below.

Email me

Or you can follow me on social media here:

IN THE CONNOR REED SERIES

The Bootneck

How far would you go for a man who gave you a second chance in life?

Bruce McQuillan leads a black operations unit only known to a handful of men.

A sinister plot involving the Russian Bratva and one of the most powerful men within the British security services threatens to engulf the Isles.

Could a criminal with an impulse for sadism be the only man McQuillan can trust?

When the ruling class commoditise the organs of the desperate, who will stop them?

When Darren O'Reilly's daughter is found murdered with her kidney extracted, he refuses to believe the police's explanation. His quest for the truth reaches the ears of Bruce McQuillan, the leader of the shadowy Chameleon Project.

As a conspiracy of seismic proportions begins to reveal itself, Bruce realizes he needs a man of exceptional skill and ruthlessness.

He needs Connor Reed.

Ares' Thirst

Can one man stop World War Three?

When a British aid worker disappears in the Crimea, the UK Government wants her back—quickly and quietly.

And Machiavellian figures are fuelling the flames of Islamic hatred towards Russia. With 'the dark edge of the world' controlled by some of the most cunning, ruthless and powerful criminals on earth, McQuillan knows he needs to send a wolf amongst the wolves before the match of global war is struck across the rough land of Ukraine.

Northern Wars

The Ryder crime family are now at war...on three fronts.

After ruthlessly dethroning his Uncle, Connor Reed must now defend the family against the circling sharks of rival criminal enterprises.

Meanwhile, Bruce McQuillan, leader of a black operations unit named The Chameleon Project, has learnt that one of the world's most brutal and influential Mafias are targeting the UK pre-BREXIT.

Counterpart

Can Connor Reed survive his deadliest mission yet?

Bruce McQuillan's plan to light the torch of war between two of the world's most powerful and ruthless Mafias has been ignited.

Can his favoured agent, Connor Reed, fan the flames without being engulfed by them?

Especially as a man every bit his equal stands on the other side.

"When there is no enemy within, the enemies outside cannot hurt you."

Reed, a leader within his own outlaw family, delights in an opportunity to punish a thug preying on the vulnerable.

However, with his target high within a rival criminal organisation, can Reed exact retribution without dragging his relatives into a bloody war.

The Puppet Master

For the first time in history, humanity has the capacity to destroy the world.

When a British scientist leads a highly proficient Japanese engineering team in unlocking the secrets to the biosphere's survival, some will stop at nothing to see the fledging technology disappear.

In the Land of the Rising Sun, can Bruce McQuillan protect the new scientific applications from the most powerful entities on earth?

And can his favoured agent Connor Reed defeat the deadliest adversary he has ever faced?

Can the Ryder clan defeat a more ruthless organization that dwarfs them in size and finance?

When the **dark hands of a blood feud** between Irish criminal organizations begin to choke civilians, and strategies to halt the evil fail, fear grips law enforcement in the United Kingdom, the Republic of Ireland and continental Europe.

When this war ensnares the Ryder clan, Connor finds with the choice between trusting the skill and mental fortitude of untested family members, along with the motives of his enemy's enemy.

Or the complete **annihilation of his family.**

Made in the USA
Columbia, SC
08 January 2024

30052481R00098